With Spirit

Josie Mae

ISBN: 979-8-9929514-3-1

Book Cover by Caravelle Creates

First Edition 2025

Author's Note

I have a deep and passionate love for all things that are simultaneously fascinating and scary. Like many others, I never skip a story time on TikTok that explores the paranormal—unless it's late at night, even I have my limits. I grew up watching more *Ghost Hunters* than was probably healthy for an easily frightened kid. I was also raised on *Scooby-Doo* (Zombie Island is a certified classic) and *Goosebumps*, two things you'll probably see some structural parallels to in *With Spirit*.

Being able to write something that mirrors so many of my favorite pieces of media while also including a lesbian romance is literally a dream come true and a passion project many years in the making.

While written with a decent amount of levity, *With Spirit* includes some heavy themes. It's a ghost story and a haunted house story, but it's also just a story about two people meeting under odd circumstances and doing paranormal investigative work together with the help of some friends. In spirit (ha-ha) of the paranormal nature of the book, a death must occur in order for there to be a ghost. Therefore, this book tackles a few subjects that might be triggering: the loss of a loved one, grief, and forms of manipulation related to those things.

Take care of yourself as needed while reading.

Preface

The *Paranormal America* series is best treated like watching 45-minute episodes of a TV show. The books all play off of each other, the stories and lives of the characters gradually unfolding over time. The novella format is an intentional choice to prioritize the investigation as opposed to the interpersonal lives of the characters. While there will be a happily ever after for Stevie and Lo eventually (this is a romance series, after all), there will be loose ends at this end of this book.

1

LO

I'm not saying that my house is haunted, but sometimes, it really feels that way. Enough to make me believe it actually is, at least.

My inability to figure out what's really going on has been terrorizing me from the first day I got the keys to my new place. Safe to say, I've become obsessed—for weeks, it's been the only thing on my mind. Every conversation loops back around to the ghost that is sometimes a ghost and other times bad wiring or creaky floors, depending on my mood. But after a long enough time, it becomes difficult to believe that *every* weird thing that happens is purely coincidence.

"I love you, but you're starting to get a little early-season Carrie Bradshaw about this," my best friend, Annalise, tells me over drinks two months after I moved in. We're out in Silver Lake, sipping on entirely average twenty-five-dollar (with tip) cocktails. It's a perfect mid-October evening. We're surrounded by exes and friends and coworkers and people we say hi to at every party, despite not remembering their names, because Los Angeles feels like a small town sometimes.

"The ghost kind of is my Mr. Big," I admit with a sigh. The signs are there—I've been talking to every single person I know about it, obsessing over it. I've been successfully making an absolute fool of myself in the process, too. I'm sure word is spreading that I've gone a little nuts.

"So you've finally settled on it being a ghost?" She takes a sip of the whiskey sour she got for free because she slept with the bartender once. It's not her fault that he thinks there's a chance that there will be a second time. There won't be. Annalise is a budding superhero franchise actress, and when those paychecks start rolling in from her most recent job, she'll be able to afford all of the drinks she could ever want.

"I don't know what it is," I say, because my research has left me still unsure. There are too many factors at play. I keep waiting for the big reveal to be something Scooby-Doo style, like the nice couple who sold me my cute, family-style home is trying to force me out.

I *know* that there has to be a logical answer. It's like they'd always say in the medical show that I was on for far too long—don't immediately think it's something extraordinary. Do everything in your power to stick to the facts and to the obvious.

But then again, the whole reason people like my ex-show so much is because things happen all the time that *are* extraordinary. And the episodes are often based on things that actually happened, too, which means unbelievable things *can* happen and *do* happen. So it's not entirely out of the realm of possibility that's what is happening to me. Logic is the only thing preventing me from fully believing my house is haunted.

It had started off slowly. I had *that* feeling—the one at the nape of my neck, an animal instinct that told me someone was watching me. But I chalked it up to moving into a new place and not being familiar with it yet. It still hasn't really started to feel like home, even two months later. It would make sense that I'd feel a little on edge.

Then, the lights started flickering in ways that couldn't possibly be attributed to faulty wiring. And things around the house began going missing.

When I first started talking about my ghost, people enthusiastically believed me. We'd bond over drinks, exchanging stories about the times they were *certain* they'd seen a ghost that one time.

But after talking about it for long enough and with just enough distress in my voice, people at parties began to realize how deeply serious it is to me. I'd see the hot girl at a party go from vaguely interested in me to saying *Oh, I think I see my friend over there. It was nice to meet you.*

"Everyone who's been inside my house and seen it also believes something is going on," I say, almost like I'm convincing myself more so than Annalise. Annalise has never judged me, never questioned me. We met what felt like a thousand years ago—three—and lived together in an apartment that was pushed up against Elysian Park up until I bought my place. As soon as we locked eyes, we both agreed it was like we'd already known each other for a lifetime.

It's the closest to a genuine love story I've experienced anywhere off-screen. While the character I played for most of my twenties always seemed to find love and could always put her pieces back together, real life me is the girl who accidentally moves into a haunted house.

"Not everyone," Annalise clarifies. "I've been over more than anyone, and I haven't experienced anything weird." She twirls her blonde hair around her pointer finger in thought. "Actually, wait. It's only been one other person who's seen something weird. And we're not even sure that was true."

My haunted house had seeped into all aspects of my life, including my ability to flirt *and* to get laid. To celebrate having my own place with no roommate to risk overhearing, I'd enthusiastically brought someone home—a friend of a friend of a friend who was in town from Germany. Rather unsexily, I spent most of the night talking about how I didn't have any proof, but I was sure there was a ghost. She'd been intrigued rather than scared—both of me and the ghost—and still agreed to come home with me despite listening to me rant for far too long. Things had been totally fine until the ghost—or whatever—started acting up: a fan randomly began rapidly spinning in my room, and a door slammed down the hall.

She'd left quickly after that, which was somewhat of a disappointment because the sex *had* been good and we'd only gotten a round and a half in before she practically ran screaming to her Uber.

I'd been so annoyed that, after I watched her car drive off, I turned to my dark, still mostly unfurnished home and said, "Can you *not*?" And when nothing else happened, I followed that up with, "Oh, so *now* you don't want to do anything?"

Like I said, I have been absolutely losing my mind over this.

"We know for sure it was true," I say, almost a little offended. "You didn't believe me when I told you?" Annalise is making me rethink my stance on whether she's doubted me or not—maybe she's just done a good job at making me think she believes me this whole time.

"I'd like the record to show that this is the *only* time I've questioned you about your ghost, and it's because we don't know this girl. She can't back it up. We've only heard about it through you, which means you're still technically the only person who has talked about seeing the ghost. You can't be your own source in this."

I groan, knowing she's right. "This is something nobody tells you about with home ownership. I can't believe I finally do something grown up, and I'm rewarded with the house from *The Conjuring*."

"The first one in the series? I don't know if it's comparable. Your ghost seems kind of chill."

"Until I try to get laid, I guess." I lean back in my barstool, sighing. Grunge music plays over the speakers, filling the silence between us and adding to the ambiance of the pseudo-dive bar we're sitting in.

"All I'm hearing is you just have to go to other people's places instead," she replies with a shrug. "I see no issue with that."

"I really do like the house," I say, but the argument feels silly considering I've gone certifiably nuts since moving in. If the previous owners or the spirits haunting the place or whatever want me out, I'm tempted to admit defeat.

But it's not like it's a rental. I *bought* the house. I put down an absurd amount of money for it. I spent what felt like hundreds of hours touring and negotiating and hiring inspectors, plural. I had people scheduled to renovate the guest bathroom in a few months.

It's *my* house. And a particularly puritan ghost isn't going to take that from me.

"Do you think I need a priest?" I ask.

"Maybe we should start with figuring out if you actually have a ghost in the house," Annalise says and then sits up straighter. "And I think I might have just the solution, actually."

2

STEVIE

I wake up to a pillow being tossed at my head.

"What the fuck, dude?" I grumble before my brain even catches up to where I am or what's going on. I pull the pillow away from my body and drop it onto the empty couch cushion next to me. "Can I help you?"

"I've been talking to you for, like, ten minutes," Andrew, my editor, says from his desk. He turns to look at me, scratching at his beard.

I run my fingers over the ridges in my cheek that had developed in the time I'd dozed off. "And it didn't strike you as odd that I wasn't responding?"

"I thought it was a refreshing change of pace that you were letting me speak instead of talking over me."

I snort out a laugh. "Never," I say. "You need me to look at something?"

"Yeah, I'd say so." He waves his arm for me to walk over to him, and I groan, lifting myself off the couch. I rub my lower back, wincing. "That thing is so lumpy, by the way."

"I might have a solution to that problem."

I'm too tired to try and make sense of what he's saying. "I don't see the connection."

"Just come look," he says.

I groan again, mostly for dramatic effect, and hover over his shoulder. Instead of directing my attention to his computer monitors like he always does, he directs my attention to his phone. He has a social media app pulled up, and it looks like he's been messaging someone.

He hands the phone off to me. "Look at who messaged us."

I take it into my hands, blinking a few times to readjust my eyes to the tiny font in front of me. "Who's Lauren Lane?"

Andrew doesn't even attempt to hide his disgust. "For someone who works in TV, I'm appalled by how little you know."

"I work in TV, not *watch* it. Especially not scripted TV," I reply. My preference had always been movies and the occasional docuseries.

I skim over her message, curious what this supposed TV star has to say to us that has Andrew so excited.

Hi! I've heard through the grapevine that you're paranormal investigators based out of LA, and I need your help. I think the house I just bought is haunted, but I haven't been able to prove it to anyone. I've admittedly never seen your show, so I don't really know how this works, but I'll take anything that you can offer. It's gotten so bad that I really think I'm starting to believe in ghosts.

"She doesn't even watch our show," I say, gesturing to the phone.

"I think the honesty is kind of nice."

"You only like when people who aren't me are honest," I say, and Andrew only offers a shrug and a nod in response. "I don't see what the big deal here is. We get messages like this all the time."

"But this is *Lauren Lane.*"

I shake my head, not understanding what the big deal is. "Okay?"

He looks at me like I'm stupid. "She's well-known to just about anyone who isn't you," Andrew says. I roll my hand, gesturing for him to go on. "She would be great exposure for the show—meaning more money and a replacement couch. We're having a hard time being seen behind the paranormal giants' shadows. We need something fresh to set us apart. A celebrity haunting will play out better on screen than that Missouri library investigation we were planning on."

I scowl. "I was looking forward to that one."

"We need this," Andrew says, more serious than I'd ever heard him. I'm surprised by his tone, but maybe I shouldn't be—he's right that it's been difficult for us to keep up. Most of the big paranormal shows have been around for a long time. Which means dedicated fanbases and funding. They're a safe bet.

Andrew and I haven't done a terrible job—we've made it to a second season and have gotten decent play on a major streaming platform. Our viewership is steady, and we've earned what some reviewers call a *dedicated cult following*. People don't recognize us on the street, but I have consistent paychecks, which is more than I could say before starting *Paranormal America*.

We've also got the added bonus of our show being cheap. Andrew and I do just about everything ourselves—other than a few fresh-out-of-college idiot interns Andrew hired—and there's no need for a writers' room or a costume budget.

Still, that sometimes isn't enough. We can get pushed off the air for any reason. If our ratings start to slip or people get bored with us, it's all over. Shows get cancelled all the time.

That thought has me asking, "You really think she's big enough?"

Andrew nods. "She definitely is."

I exhale through my nose, thinking it over. "Okay. I like the plan. But I think you're forgetting the biggest piece in all of this."

"What?"

I look at Andrew like he's lost his mind. "We're a TV show, dude. She clearly wants an actual paranormal investigator, not a bunch of people with camera equipment and a background in practical effects."

Andrew sits quietly in his office chair for a beat. "I mean, we've both acted. We can keep the bit up for the sake of the show, right? And she seems pretty certain the house is actually haunted, which means we'll probably have some stuff to film. It'd be kind of cool to become an actual ghost-hunting show instead of a fake one."

I roll my eyes. I don't know how Andrew can be wrapped up in this show and still believe in anything paranormal. We've been to so many different abandoned and presumably haunted places, and the only sightings we've ever had have been designed by us.

"When she figures out that it's fake, it'll be over for us. Our credibility will be shot," I say, propping myself against the ledge of his desk. "A lot of people already kind of know the truth about shows like ours, but no one wants the fun to be ruined. It's like Santa. Doing an episode with someone who thinks we're legitimate is way too risky."

Andrew's expression doesn't change. I can tell he's dead set on this. "We'll just have to do a really good job, I guess, because I already told her we'd come"

3

LO

Within one week of my messaging the *Paranormal America* team, they scheduled a time to come to my house to shoot. Paperwork was signed, a pair of boys no older than twenty-two scoped the place out for filming, and we were set to begin, all before I could even fully process what was going on.

"Have you met Stevie yet?" Annalise asks. We're both sitting on the couch in my living room, waiting for the lead investigators on the show to come by for my first filmed interview for the show. Nearly everything is set up and good to go. I did my hair and makeup like I normally do and put on similar clothes to what I always wear. I don't view this as going on TV to the degree that I need to be dressed up; I view this as a somewhat embarrassing cry for help.

"No, not yet." When Annalise had recommended looking into *Paranormal America* that night at the bar, I'd done a little digging before messaging them.

Stevie is objectively hot. She has the lethal combination of great bone structure, great hair, and a great screen presence. The clips I watched of her were admittedly compelling, even as someone who'd never gotten into the whole paranormal TV show thing.

"I think she's going to be even hotter in person," Annalise says, as if she can read my mind.

I'm mostly unaffected. Annalise and I see beautiful people all the time; it's part of our work. And if I've learned anything in my time of living in a haunted house and telling people about it, people don't tend to find it sexy when you're at the end of your rope. It doesn't matter if I find Stevie hot since she's almost definitely not going to be interested in a woman on the verge, anyway.

The doorbell rings out—a soft, beautiful series of notes—and I get up to go meet Stevie and whoever else she has with her.

When I open the door, I realize immediately that perhaps I underestimated Stevie's looks a little too much. I blink at her, barely registering that she has other people by her side.

She keeps her brunette hair in an intentionally mussed wolf cut. Her green eyes are wide and perceptive, brushing over me and hovering for only a second on my face. Silver chains sit flat against her chest. Unsurprisingly, she wears all black—the perfect stylistic choice for someone who's a little edgy and works in the paranormal. I can't help but admire the commitment to branding.

"Can we come in?" she asks impatiently—and even a little rudely. It immediately breaks the spell she has on me; she's just another person in entertainment I could find hot but I absolutely should not get involved with.

I step to the side, and her colleague from the show offers me an apologetic smile. "I'm Andrew, that's Stevie. She's...efficient," he explains.

"I'm used to it," I say as Stevie and Andrew make their way into my home. And it's true—I am. Despite the California-cool stereotype, the entertainment industry is a completely different beast. Everything is serious, and time is quite literally money. Stevie is just one of a million producers who skip niceties for the sake of getting things done.

I look around at what they're seeing for the first time—the boxes I still haven't unpacked, the empty spots in my entry way and living room where art and personal items should be. It's been a slow and intentional process getting moved in. I'd rather take my time finding things I like than rush to fill the space.

But now that my house is about to be the featured location of a TV show, I'm regretting the decision to pace myself. I've been on camera for most of my life, so I don't care about myself on screen, but I've never done an interview in my own place before. It feels strangely intimate.

"Sorry about..." I gesture at my house.

"We're not *Architectural Digest,* we don't care," Stevie responds as she pulls a dining room chair into the living room to sit on. I can't tell if I find her response comforting or dismissive.

"You have a beautiful home," Andrew says, and I offer him a polite smile.

"Hi," Annalise says from the couch. "Annalise."

"Andrew, nice to meet you," he says, walking over to her to shake her hand. Stevie only offers a glance and a nod of acknowledgement.

For the first time since messaging them, I wonder if maybe this was all a mistake. Maybe this is too far. Maybe there isn't a ghost in my house, and I've just been making it up this entire time.

But then I think about how I only slept five hours last night because my living room TV kept turning on and off, and I know for certain this is for the best. Ghost or not, I can't handle this on my own.

"How long have you guys been doing this? Like, ghost hunting or whatever?" Annalise asks. She turns and looks at me, mouthing, *Hot!* before turning back to Stevie.

"Oh, you know," Stevie says, which doesn't really feel like an answer, but maybe it's an obvious one. We'd probably know if we'd ever actually watched their show.

I sit down on the couch as Stevie and Andrew fiddle with their equipment.

"I'm glad nothing got broken overnight," I say, looking at all the lighting and sound equipment they'd left here.

"Yeah," Stevie says. Yet another noncommittal answer. What the hell was her problem?

"Is your ghost...active?" Andrew asks. He sounds almost a little nervous, which I didn't expect from someone who'd been going into haunted places for pay for at least one season of television. I admittedly didn't look into Andrew or Stevie beyond that, so I have no idea how long either of them has actually been paranormal investigators.

"Yeah. She makes herself known," I say.

"You know it's a she?" Stevie asks.

"Oh, I don't know. I'm just guessing. The stuff the ghost is doing doesn't feel particularly...aggressive, I guess. Mostly just lights flickering. No threats or anything. At least, not yet. I'd imagine those to be mostly male-ghost behaviors, but maybe I'm stereotyping."

Stevie shrugs. "They can run the gambit."

She throws herself down onto the chair across from me coolly, and Andrew gets to work on the camera and adjusting the lighting around me. The other two boys on their crew come in and out to help.

I'm used to shows having what feels like a million people around me at all times on set, so it's weird for it to be so quiet. The closeness makes me uneasy. All over again. I'm regretting my decision to go on camera to talk about this, but it's definitely too late now.

It also doesn't help that Stevie has a kind of magnetism that makes it hard not to stare at her. I feel an annoying urge to impress her. She's been nothing but off-putting, but I keep finding myself turning my attention her way as she moves around the room to check equipment and the way my living room looks on camera.

"Alright, let's get this moving. The light is good right now," Stevie says and sits down in my chair to face me on the couch. "We're going to start with just having you on camera."

I nod, and Annalise gives me a thumbs-up from her spot on the couch.

Stevie glances down at the clipboard in her lap, one of her legs propped up on the other one to form a confident square.

"Thanks for doing this," Stevie says

I'm so caught off guard by the earnestness that I don't have the time to formulate a response before Andrew starts rolling. Stevie and I watch him for our cue.

Once Stevie gets the go-ahead, she turns back to look at me. "How's your day going?"

"Oh, it's okay," I say. I know this is just her way of loosening me up before interviewing me, but I appreciate it. Despite my years of practice with interviews, my palms are slick with sweat. I'm uncharacteristically nervous; I can hear it in the slight shake of my voice, and I can't get myself to sit still. I wasn't even this nervous for the Emmys.

I don't know if it's because of Stevie or because it feels strange to go on record about something other than my career, but I can't dwell on it on camera. I have to talk my way through the nerves, just like I used to do when I was early in my career and every audition felt like life or death. "I was kept up all last night. I think the ghost knew you were coming."

Stevie's lips turn up in an amused smile just for me to see. My heart flutters in a way that is totally unwelcome. Despite my efforts to not be won over by Stevie, I don't think this is a battle I'm going to win. Even Annalise would say *so what if she's awful? You can still fuck* and that is not helpful in this moment. "Is that something you've gotten used to?"

"It's been a trend. Things get...weird when there's a change in routine."

"Tell me more about that."

Somewhat annoyingly, having Stevie's undivided attention sends butterflies fluttering through my stomach. Now isn't the time for butterflies; this is serious.

"A lot of things happen here that don't seem particularly paranormal, but they also don't feel normal, either," I explain. The camera and the people hovering around my living room disappear as I just focus on telling my story to Stevie. "My electricity flickers a lot. Things like a TV turning on and off seem more like it's about the house than a ghost, but it happens all the time. And no one has found anything wrong with any of my wiring."

"Odd," Stevie says, and I nod in agreement. "Have you seen anything? Or anyone?"

"I haven't actually *seen* anything, but I've felt the presence of someone else in the room with me," I say, carefully choosing my words. "I'll just be, like, cooking or something and just...feel it."

Stevie leans forward in her chair, her green eyes captivating me. "Do you believe in ghosts, Lauren Lane?"

My name on her lips sends an unfortunate flush through me—a reminder that my sex life has suffered in the time since I moved in. "I think what's been going on here is enough to make me believe in them."

4

STEVIE

Before meeting Lauren Lane—or *Lo* as she introduced herself—Andrew insisted on giving me a very thorough rundown of her background: She's an actress who starred on a soapy medical drama for eight seasons, she has a massive following of adoring fans who consider her a fan favorite, and she's well-connected in our industry.

"She's also publicly a lesbian and has been single for some time," Andrew had said on the drive over to her house. I half-sighed, half-groaned when he glanced over at me. I couldn't tell if he was giving me a warning not to flirt with her, or warning me that she might try to make a move. Either was a possibility; Andrew had seen more than a few women over the years stumble through making a pass at me.

"That usually just means she hasn't been seen publicly with anyone. Girls like her don't stay unattached for very long. I'm sure she has a long line of potential suitors," I'd responded.

"So you agree she's beautiful?"

The few pictures I'd seen of her flashed back into my mind. Long blonde hair, a wide movie star smile. When she's not made up for TV, she has freckles across the bridge of her nose. Her eyes are a warm hazel with the kind of depth that comes across even in pictures.

"She's alright," I said and slugged back the rest of my hot coffee.

The conversation plays out in my head when I see Lo in person for the first time. But I don't date. I don't have the time for serious commitment, and I'm not interested in having anyone waiting at home for me when I get back from shooting on location somewhere. That doesn't stop me from admitting to myself that Lo is someone I would hit on at a bar.

It also, unfortunately, plays out the entire time I'm interviewing her. I'm fighting off two parts of my brain—the first keeps worrying someone will slip up and we'll be revealed as frauds to Lo, and the second is so focused on the way her lips form words that I'm worried I'll forget how to speak.

After listening to Lo talk for long enough, though, I start to get lost in her story. The way she speaks and tells stories is mesmerizing.

And the way she's so distressed makes me feel a little bad for developing an entire TV show around fake paranormal encounters. Outside of a few stories my grandparents told me growing up—which were definitely just folklore, anyway—I'd never met anyone with a ghost story they really believed. I'm not necessarily convinced Lo's house is really haunted, but I do believe her fear is real.

"And you don't know anything about the history of the house?" I ask.

She offers a modest half-shrug. "No, not really. It hasn't crossed my mind to check. I think I've been so caught up in figuring out if what I'm experiencing is real that I haven't even done any investigative work. I think I've mostly been trying to convince myself that I'm losing my mind and none of this is real. Doing research makes it feel real."

"Are you looking forward to learning more about the house?" I ask. As part of our show, we offer a historical background of whatever place it is we're 'investigating.' We've gotten creative with making it up in some places but with Lo, Andrew and I agreed we wanted to do it right. No embellishing, no feeding people lines—just a real and true ghost story. Or an episode about how her house isn't actually haunted, which is the more likely alternative.

"I'm a little nervous to look into it, to be honest." Lo sits with her thoughts for a second. Her brow furrows with genuine worry. "What if something horrible happened here?"

"It'll be alright. Whatever happened would've been a long time ago," I assure her.

"But isn't the whole point of, like, ghost hunting that...*things* can live in places forever? Sometimes people don't leave? Or can't?"

Shit.

"To a certain extent," I offer, trying to sound more confident than I'm feeling. I'm not used to having to talk without some kind of set script—or without the people around me knowing that it's all bullshit. Talking out my ass doesn't work here. But saying things that suggest I don't even believe in ghosts—because I don't and never have—isn't going to go over well here. It'll put us on the fast track to Lo seeing right through us.

"Right," Lo says. Her eyes don't leave my face and I worry that she's already somehow onto us.

We wrap up our initial questions, mostly just baiting for her sound clips. She's doing a good job of selling the story. Better than when Andrew and I draft something up quickly for us to say or for someone else to say. We don't do formal scripts for the show, but we usually have soundbites that we want to capture, mostly for promotional purposes.

Andrew and I have good practice with feeding people lines; after scaring myself out of thinking I was good enough for features, I've stuck to reality TV. After doing a few dating shows—one of which was where I met Andrew—we pitched our own show using the skills we already have, but in a way that no longer felt evil. Neither of us really thought it would work, but we've had a lot of fun doing it, and it's paid better so far than anything else we've done.

"She just doesn't want to scare you. Don't worry until there's something to worry about," Andrew offers from across the room. He's getting the camera set up over his shoulder so we can do the walkthrough of the house with Lo. Everything after this point is pretty casual—one camera that goes with me and Andrew, and then some random cameras we'll place around the house.

"Exactly," I say, grateful for the out. I make a mental note to buy Andrew an entire bottle of whiskey as a thank you for saving my ass.

"Have you guys seen the second lav mic?" Andrew asks, glancing over at our interns for assistance. They look at him blankly, like it's their first day on earth.

"Did you pack it?" I ask.

"Yeah, it never goes anywhere without the other," he says. He looks around at all of the equipment we have laid out. We've made a mess of Lo's dining room. There are open boxes for our equipment, coffees, and copies of the shooting schedule. "Shit, dude. I just bought those new replacement ones, too."

"It's probably just caught up in the rest of the stuff." I wave our two interns, Sean and Tanner—or affectionately tweedle-dee and tweedle-dum because they're twenty-one-year-old twin boys who would forget their heads if they weren't attached—over. "Can you help Andrew look? Did you guys pack them up by accident?"

Tweedle-dum shook his head. "Man, I don't think so," he says, looking over the rest of the table. He scratches the back of his neck, where his mullet meets his bare skin. "Um."

"I can help look," Lo says.

"It's alright. This happens sometimes," I say.

"Not really, if I'm going to be honest." He groans, uncharacteristically more stressed about this snafu than I was. But he'd also always been our equipment guy; every piece of tech we owned was his baby. "Those things were expensive, dude."

"It's literally fine."

"It's probably gone," Lo offers ominously.

That makes the rest of the room pause.

"What do you mean?" I ask even though I'm not sure I really want to know the answer. I don't get freaked out because I don't believe in this stuff, but Lo's tone is so grim it feels like the set-up for a horror movie. And personally, I've never been interested in being a final girl, especially not against some kind of paranormal entity.

"It was like I was saying, things go missing here all the time." She explains this like it's the most obvious thing in the world, so matter-of-fact that I know this isn't the first time. "I'd initially told myself that the things I was missing had just gotten packed in the boxes I hadn't opened yet. And then when I opened all of the boxes, I told myself the movers probably forgot one or one got put in a weird spot of the house. But then other things that I know made it to the house went missing."

"But you've found them, right?" Andrew asks. "Since then?"

She shakes her head. "No, I haven't. I had an entire bag of winter attire, like hats and scarves and whatever else, I was going to repack and then hide in a closet for my next ski trip. But I literally haven't been able to find it anywhere."

The hair on the back of my neck stands up. I've always been a skeptic, always the asshole who shoots down ghost stories or pokes holes in myths, but I'm not liking Lo's tone. When she was just telling us her story, it felt different. But now, it feels more like a warning. Or a threat.

"Have you seen anything weird here?" I ask, directing my attention to Lo's friend. She'd been suspiciously quiet about her own feelings about Lo's house.

"Oh, none of us have seen anything other than Lo," she says. She has her legs folded up under her on a loveseat, her eyes fixed on her phone. "I believe her, but I'm not interested in engaging. If there's a ghost, it's not my business."

Lo shrugs. "And I mean, it could always just be moving stress. People misplace things all the time."

"How long ago did you move in again?" Andrew asks.

"Two months," she says. "Just over, at this point."

"And you have things you haven't been able to find in all that time?"

"Andrew, can you come grab something from the van with me?" I cut in, interrupting the conversation. Hopefully, Lo can't hear the edge of panic in my voice.

"Sure," he says. His eyes dance around the house as he walks across the living room toward me.

"Can you hurry up?" I say through my teeth.

"Sorry," he says and picks up the pace.

"We'll be back in a second. We're going to check if the mic was just left behind in the car."

"Take your time," Lo says. When I look back at her, the expression on her face tells me she doesn't expect we'll find it. It sends a shiver down my spine.

When we leave out the front door, I nearly drag Andrew by his shirt collar to keep up pace with me. We follow the path of flowers lining the pavement, cutting back down to the street. Unsurprisingly, Lo lives in one of the few neighborhoods of Los Angeles that has wide streets and beautiful, healthy trees. Even though it looks like my parents' house, tucked deep in the suburbs of West Pennsylvania, I know it cost her five times what my parents ever paid.

I lean against the van and look at him. "What is wrong with you?"

"I don't like whatever is going on in that house," Andrew says. "I have a weird feeling, dude. Like a really weird one."

"She's just telling you a scary story. People lose things all the time. Imagine if you blamed a ghost every time you misplaced your keys. It's ridiculous."

Andrew doesn't seem convinced. He looks back at the house like it's an animal preying on him.

"Are you seriously telling me you believe her?" I ask, lightly hitting my hand against Andrew's chest. "Ghosts aren't real. Our entire show is proving to both of us that it's all bullshit."

"This feels different."

"Does it? Or is an actress just doing a really good job of convincing you that she thinks her house is haunted?" I ask.

"There's probably some very reasonable explanation behind all of this, just like there always is."

Andrew takes a deep breath through his nose. "I don't want to stay here too late tonight."

"Bummer. We work for a ghost hunting show and literally can't film our most important scenes during the day," I say. My patience is growing increasingly thin with him. We don't have time to fuck around like this; we have a job to do. "Need I remind you that *you* were the one who wanted to take this episode on?"

He's quiet for a long beat and then finally says, "You're right."

"We're good to film now? Think you can handle it?" I ask.

"Yeah," Andrew says, even though he still looks uneasy. The one pass that I'll give him is that this is the first place we're filming where someone is telling us actual—or supposed—-firsthand accounts of paranormal activity. Typically, we intentionally choose places that are rumored to be haunted or look like they could be haunted and then fill in the blanks ourselves. We have people in town talk to us, edit what they have to say during their interviews to be as eerie as possible, or set them up to give us quotes we want, and then construct our own ghost encounters. We usually have full control over the situation. But here, someone isn't just saying, *Yeah, it's definitely creepy here.* Lo is explicitly telling us ghost stories.

But I can only give him so much of a pass considering he's the one who wanted to take a chance on Lo. And he also willingly signed on to be on a paranormal investigation show.

"Okay, great," I say. I start heading back toward the house, walking backwards with my eyes on him. I make it a few paces up the driveway before turning back toward him. "Are you coming?"

Andrew scrunches his face in reluctance.

"I literally can't do this show without you. We'll be done in, like, an hour, and then we'll go to the library to film and then wrap tomorrow. We're so close to being done."

"We haven't even gotten to the actual ghost stuff in the house."

"You and I both know that's not bad. We'll film for a few hours tomorrow night and edit it to look like we've been there all night, and it'll be fine," I say. When Andrew doesn't budge from the street, I sigh. "This job isn't any different from the other ones we've worked. I promise. If all it takes for you to believe a place is haunted is that things flicker and go missing, you're so gullible I can't believe you've made it this far."

Andrew groans and rolls his neck. "Alright. Whatever. Fine."

"Great, thank you." It comes out sounding more agitated than grateful. But it's valid of me—I can't deal with this shit right now. We have a job to do. And we have a whole season to go. I can't have my guys starting to think that ghosts really exist. All of these—admittedly creepy, but definitively *not* haunted—places that we typically film are about to be a lot less straightforward than they have been in the past.

In the time that we were standing outside, the sun quickly began setting on us. Every fall and winter, it surprises me how suddenly the daylight fades. As we're inching toward November, every day feels shorter and shorter, getting darker and darker earlier each day.

I know the sudden dark isn't going to help my case with getting Andrew to calm down, but it's not my fault he's falling victim to an actress. If anything, she's not even being particularly convincing. She could definitely go harder if given the opportunity. I would bet money that there will be hundreds of posts about this episode online, saying that Lo is a terrible actress and no one believes her house is actually haunted. People love to poke holes in our episodes; it's part of the gig.

When we step up to the front door, the outdoor light flickers and fades. It takes a long time to finally stay fully lit up. Andrew lets out something like a whimper behind me.

"See, faulty wiring," I say, gesturing up toward the light. "Nothing weird."

I push open the door and am immediately swallowed up by a weird feeling—a cold breeze, a swirling in my stomach that tells me to get out. Goosebumps bloom over my arms.

"Jesus Christ," Andrew mutters from behind me and I don't have to ask to know he just experienced the same thing. What I can't tell is if he meant that as an expletive or as a prayer.

"I'm sure the air conditioning is on, whatever," I say, brushing it off again—this time a little less certain than before. LA stays warm well into October during the day, but the evenings cool down significantly. There's no need for air conditioning right now.

Now that the warm sunset is fading, the house has gone mostly dark. The little light left comes in through the windows. In the living room, Lo had turned on a few random lamps around the room.

“You don’t believe in overhead lighting?” I ask.

She wrinkles her nose. “I’m offended you’d even ask,” she says. Ah, go it. She’s one of those *the big light is evil* types.

I scoff. “No wonder you think there’s a ghost living here. The vibe is…” I look around at how the lamp creates shadows around the room. Again, that feeling like I just stepped into a horror movie sets in. This time, it’s *Scream*—a killer peering in through the windows from the outside, motion detected at the front door, and then the back door, and an unwelcome phone call. *I see you*.

I shake off the thought. This house is just like any other house. There’s nothing weird going on. Nothing has changed inside just because the light is fading.

“It’s meant to be cozy,” Lo says. “But it doesn’t really feel that cozy here for some reason.”

“I have to agree. The vibe is pretty abysmal,” Annalise says and finally puts her phone down. “There’s a reason no one wants to hang out here after dark.”

Lo gasps with offense. “You told me the house didn’t scare you!”

“I didn’t want to scare you more by telling you that the house definitely has a fucked up energy,” she says. “I love you too much to ruin your new house for you. But now that you have these guys here, hopefully we can figure out a solution."

"You know that we don't, like, get rid of ghosts, right? We just monitor to figure out if they're here?" I say.

Annalise waves me off. "It's fine. If we find out that there definitely isn't anything weird going on here, we can move on. We'll just chalk it up to the house feeling a little off-putting and buy Lo some more furniture."

"I'm buying at my own pace. I'm trying to *curate*," she says.

Even though I've never once put any thought into decorating my apartments, I can't help but be charmed by Lo's answer.

Annalise's lips turn up in a smile. "Of course. In the way only you can," she says good-naturedly. "Should we get moving on touring the house? I'm sure you want at least a little natural light for this part."

The rest of Lo's house is about as half-empty as the living room and entryway. Every room is nicely put together with obvious thought behind the color coordination and a consistent mid-century inspired theme through the house, but there isn't much to see other than that. We've shot literal abandoned buildings with more furniture than this.

Andrew—holding the camera—and I follow Lo as she gives us an overall tour. "This is the primary. Sometimes when I'm in here, I can hear what sounds like footsteps outside the door," she explains, just like I'd asked her to do. The entire house has been one thing after another—items getting moved from where she knows she put them, a door cracked that she didn't open, a weirdly cold breeze in a windowless bathroom.

"*Eesh*," Andrew says in response to her comment about the footsteps, and I turn to glare at him. "Sorry."

"You guys aren't very into ghosts for being ghost investigators, are you?" Lo asks, turning the attention briefly away from the tour she's giving us. She stands at the doorframe to her bedroom, which is the most complete room of the entire house. She has beautiful dark wood furniture and a surprisingly massive collection of books. It feels like a library she happens to sleep in. "You're both being weird."

"Not being weird," I protest.

"I'm getting the sense you guys are more scared of my house than I am, and I'm not sure I like that." She crosses her arms across her chest, and I feel a little bit like a kid who's about to get caught in a lie by my teacher.

"It's a little creepier here than we're used to, I guess," I say, shooting another pointed glare in Andrew's direction. "Most of the places we tour are abandoned or old or whatever. It's weird that all of this stuff is happening *here*, where you live."

"A little too close to home, too," Andrew says.

"It's not like ghosts are contagious. I'm sure there are like a thousand other places in LA that are haunted, people just don't talk about it," Lo says. "Or I guess maybe you guys would know those places already. But you know what I mean."

I turn to her. "You're really not scared? I know I'm not, but I have experience with this," I add. A little white lie won't hurt anyone. "You're surprisingly pretty...calm."

"I guess I keep thinking there's some kind of explanation," she says with a half-shrug. "Whether it's me being naive or what, I don't know. But I'm sooner ready to believe that someone is like, playing a prank on me or something, than to believe my house is actually haunted. Even with all of the weird stuff that goes on here."

"Fair," I say, admittedly impressed by her ability to stay level-headed through all of this. Something about it makes me almost believe her more; it feels almost like how I'd approach it if I thought my own apartment was haunted. I'd think through every logical explanation, and even when logic didn't seem to offer any answers, I'd still cling to that before I'd jump to believing it's a ghost.

"But, yeah, that's the tour. Nothing much else to say," she says. Just then, the lights do the same thing they did outside—flicker but in a distinctive way, like someone is dimming them and then turning them all the way up. It makes the hair on even the back of *my* neck stand up—it's almost like it's moving in a pattern. Flickering from one end, progressively down the hallway until it's above us.

The thought hits me like a truck: it doesn't feel like how a light typically flickers when there's an issue with the house itself. It feels intentional.

Or like someone—or something—just walked down the hallway, setting the lights off in the process.

"Absolutely the fuck not," Andrew mutters under his breath. He looks over at me like he's waiting for me to give him permission to run. If Lo wasn't standing right in front of us, I'd snap at him for being a moron and nearly blowing our cover. But since Lo is right there—and already seems a little skeptical of us—I keep my annoyance at bay.

"She's saying hi," Lo says simply, an amused smile turning her lips upward.

"Does that happen a lot?" I ask. Despite wanting to wring Andrew's neck for acting like a little bitch, I'm also not feeling particularly cool about what just happened. My heart rate is sky high, my palms sweaty. I'm experiencing the kind of post-adrenaline I'd only ever experienced after watching a horror movie.

"I mean, yeah," Lo says. She gestures to the house. "I'm used to it. Just like I already told you every other time you've asked me a variation of that question. It's my house. I bought it. I'm going to keep living in it and do the best I can to make it feel normal."

I think through every logical explanation, telling myself that there's a reason behind all of this. It's the house. There's no ghost, no outlandish explanation. I've gone a long time without ever truly being convinced the paranormal exists; I'm not about to start now.

"Did you get everything you needed here?" Lo asks.

"Definitely," Andrew responds for both of us.

5

LO

After saying my goodbye to Annalise for the evening—she's booked out for the night with a screening of a friend's movie—I followed behind Stevie and Andrew's van all the way to the library. We aren't going to the local one that I sometimes stop into whenever the books I already own aren't speaking to me; instead, the *Paranormal America* team reserved a late-evening filming slot at the largest library in the county.

It's dark now, but it feels better on the road than it did at my house. I'm too proud to admit it to Stevie—I've been enjoying being better equipped at handling ghosts than paranormal investigators—but my house does scare me at night. Not enough to want to leave and go somewhere else, but enough to unsettle me. My nighttime routine consists of making sure I'm in my bedroom with the door locked before eight p.m. as many nights as possible.

It's a silly attempt at protection since it feels like an obvious truth that ghosts can just go through walls whenever they want.

But it makes me feel better, since I really don't know for sure there *is* a ghost in my house.

But I am feeling a little vindicated that not only did people other than me have paranormal experiences in my house, but it was all caught on camera. *And* Stevie and Andrew—about as expert as someone can be at something like spotting a ghost—seem to think there's something paranormal going on.

After finding street parking a few spots down from the *Paranormal America* van—a giant black one with their logo covering the entire right side—I walk down the sidewalk to meet them.

"Hey." I raise my voice slightly so it'll carry to them over the light city noise around us. The air feels different here than it does inside my house, like it always does. Being forty minutes away from my place—the Los Angeles equivalent of a quick ten-minute drive down the road—lifts a weight off my chest.

Stevie greets me with a slight head nod. "Have you been to this library before?"

"I don't usually come downtown, honestly," I say. "Too far and too much traffic."

"Spoken like a true Los Angeleno," Stevie agrees. "I dated a girl in Culver for a while, and it was basically a long-distance relationship."

I brush off the feeling that Stevie mentioning an ex stirs up in me. The image I have in my head of her did not include any actual exes, just a long list of conquests. But it's stupid of me to feel even a little bit jealous. "You live downtown?"

"I do, but I try to spend as little time at home as possible. Home means I'm not working."

"Spoken like a true Los Angeleno," I echo, and Stevie's lips turn up in a small smile that makes me feel annoyingly victorious. I hate that I want her approval. It's the curse of meeting someone hot: it doesn't matter who you are, how successful you are, how beautiful you are—a hot person wanting you is the only validation that seems to really mean anything.

Or at least, that's how it's always been for me. But that's also coming from someone whose first kiss was on screen and didn't have a crush like me back until I got on a wildly popular TV show as an adult.

"Alright, let's get it," Stevie says and heads up the sidewalk toward two outdoor staircases. They lead to a building with no identifying information, at least in the low light of the evening. It's completely tucked away from this angle.

"This is the library?" I ask, surprised.

"Yeah, it looks a little cooler from the other side, but this is where the good street parking usually is," Stevie explains. "It also looks a little better during the day. It's kind of creepy at night."

We head up the stairs and up toward the massive front entrance doors. When we go inside, it starts to look a little more like a library. The familiar scent of books and the sweetness of lingering perfumes from throughout the day feel like coming home.

Despite being there just before closing, it's still pretty busy. It makes sense why there are so many people around—the library is massive. It's easily the biggest library I've ever seen. From the lobby, hallways extend out in all directions. Various entrances and exits, side rooms identified for teaching, and different sections based on the genre of interest. It's nothing like the library I'd grown up with, which was basically just one very large room. This seems to go on forever.

"I love it here," I admit.

"Yeah, you would," Stevie says, and when she sees the expression on my face, she furrows her brow slightly. "I saw the books in your room. This is probably every reader's paradise. I've just always been more of a movie person."

She then walks off like that wasn't the nicest thing I'd heard her say over the several hours I'd spent in close proximity with her.

I think I'm starting to understand the rhythm of her communication style and the kind of person she is. But then again, it seems like Stevie is someone who's full of surprises, even when she doesn't mean to be.

Stevie and Andrew lead me down one of the hallways, and we head into a massive room with tall ceilings and windows on top of windows.

"Oh my god," I mutter under my breath.

"Cool, right?" Stevie says.

We step onto an escalator—I can't even believe a library in the world is large enough to justify an escalator, nonetheless *several*—and head up.

"The woman who runs the archives is pretty cool. We haven't shot a ton in LA, but she's hooked us up in other cities. Librarians are surprisingly well-connected."

It's annoying how hot it is to hear Stevie praising librarians. It doesn't exactly align with her cool-girl attitude to be nice to them, and the surprise makes it all the better. I can't tell if I'm relieved she's a good person, or annoyed because it means I can't use it as a reason to write her off. Either way, I feel like I'm losing.

Or maybe winning. But only if Stevie feels similarly intrigued by me—which is not a vibe I've gotten so far.

"Cool," I say, a beat too late because I was too busy stealing glances at Stevie's full lips.

When we make it to the top of the escalator, offering a full view of the several stories of the library below us, Stevie opens the door to a side room with glass walls. There's a sign up on the glass that says *Closed for Filming!*

"Thank you," I say as I step through.

"Ah, Stevie! Andrew! Welcome!" a woman with streaks of gray through beautiful chestnut hair greets us. She offers a wide smile and readjusts her giant, thick-framed glasses. She's standing behind a massive circular desk, piles of books surrounding her. "And we have a new friend this time. How's your ghost treating you?"

"Not particularly well, but we're coexisting." She throws her head back with a laugh.

"I'm Farrah. I'm part of the History Department staff here at the library. You guys will be looking at *my* personal favorite section, which is the California Index."

"Dr. Houston is very knowledgeable about the history of Southern California," Stevie offers.

Farrah brushes off the comment with a smile. "Too nice to me," she says. "We're just excited to have the opportunity to share our archives with you. We get a decent amount of foot traffic, but not as much as the other sections of the libraries."

"Excited to be here," I say.

"You know where to go?" Farrah asks.

"Yeah, we're good," Andrew answers politely, a smile also on his face.

"Alright, let me know if you need anything," she says.

Stevie gestures for me to follow her. Andrew and I head back into a far corner of the archives. The deeper we go, the darker it gets. If I hadn't already been living in a supposed haunted house, this would send shivers down my spine. It's eerily quiet and isolated—just us and books and low lighting for what feels like forever.

Eventually, we make it to the furthest possible wall in the room. I turn back and can't even see Dr. Houston anymore. There aren't any windows this way, and I can't tell if that's intentional for the books or a design choice.

Machines I don't recognize line one of the walls, and I frown. "These are for microfilms. I don't think the history of your house will go back so far that we'll need them, but we'll see," Stevie says when she sees me looking at the machines.

"They look good on camera, so we might get some b-roll using them," Andrew says. "Even if we don't actually end up needing them."

"Cool," I say, as if I'm not freaking out a tiny bit at getting to see this part of the library. "I had no idea this was here."

"Most people don't," Andrew says as he sets up his camera. The shoot is obviously meant to be casual—it's just him with his camera and some lighting. I haven't seen a setup this casual since I was in film school and working on sets for student projects.

"What's the budget for an episode?" I ask. "Genuinely curious."

"Even lower than you're probably imagining," Stevie admits.

"And people like this? All of the ghost hunting stuff?" I ask.

Stevie snorts out a laugh as she helps Andrew get the lighting set up. "I mean, yeah. It's not a bad market. It's pretty hit or miss, especially against the big dogs of the industry. But if you can keep it interesting, people will tune in."

"Do you have goals for it?" I ask. My face flushes a burning hot red. "Sorry, I don't mean for this to be twenty questions. I'm just curious."

"I guess our goal would be wider production. The more money that flows into the show, the more we can do and the more money that comes toward us. It's kind of a win all around.

But the lifespan of a show right now, even with a cheap budget, is short, as I'm sure you know."

"All too well," I answer with a sigh. After leaving the medical show I was on for seven years—I was killed off in a devastating hospital fire—it's been hard to gain footing elsewhere. I've shot some pilots, worked here and there. Fortunately, the money can really stretch far with residuals and the fact that I'm pretty low maintenance. Some inherited family money doesn't hurt, either.

But that can only go on for so long. My agent has been hard at work doing whatever she can for me. We're hoping something will stick eventually, but it's always a surprise. There are pilots that don't get picked up, shows that only last a season, and roles I land that are for brief arcs that don't get extended.

The worst part is that it's hard not working and having something to keep me occupied. It was also hard while I was working—shooting schedules are intense and long and will happen at all hours of the day—but this is a different kind of challenge.

Initially, having the break from work felt like the perfect excuse to focus on myself and my house and take a deep breath. But my house being haunted kind of ruined that for me, and now, all I want is any excuse to be *out* of my house.

"Alright," Stevie says. "What's your address again? Let's see what we can find."

After giving my information over to Stevie, she went to work on pulling everything she could. Newspaper clippings, information on former home ownership. Anything that mentioned my street or my address—and then also anything mentioning the names of the people who lived at that address—was pulled up online and printed or pulled from a book.

"I guess I should've done more research before buying," I say, looking over what Stevie found. I've mostly just been twiddling my thumbs while she's gone to work, watching the back of her head and the way her hands look typing on a keyboard. I'm sure Andrew—who was testing the lighting and adjusting the camera around me—caught me looking over at Stevie more than once.

"This actually isn't bad," she says as she sits down in the chair across from me. The entire history of my house is laid out in the middle of us. "Some of the other places we've looked at have had a lot more history, especially the really old and abandoned ones. You'd be surprised how many news clippings there are about places people aren't even supposed to go into anymore."

"Fair enough," I say.

"This part is pretty simple; we're just going to review everything together. Catch earnest reactions to reading things. That kind of thing."

I bite my lip. "What if we find something?" I ask, repeating my question from earlier. But the concern is still there, sitting in the pit of my stomach.

"Honestly, the bigger concern is what if there *isn't* anything," Stevie says. "With the...state of your house, so to speak, wouldn't it be kind of nice to have some kind of answer?"

"Not to question your line of work, but isn't chalking it up to *I have a ghost in my house* not exactly an answer?"

Stevie shrugs. "Depends on who you ask." She turns to Andrew. "You're good. Start rolling."

I square off my shoulders instinctively, second-nature with how much time I've spent in front of a camera over the years, and wait for Andrew's signal.

"Okay, so the basics—your house was built in 1969. One bedroom, one bath. Tucked into a quiet neighborhood," Stevie says, reading off some of the papers she found.

"Sounds right."

"Idyllic."

"Some would say."

"So, the owners who sold it to you had only owned the house for about four years before handing it off to you," Stevie says, and I nod to confirm. "I'm assuming they didn't mention anything about ghosts?

"No, nothing out of the ordinary came up. But I also never met the owners. Everything was handled through realtors."

"Did the realtor tell you anything about the owners before them?"

I shook my head. "I never asked."

"It looks like Irene Bevere, who owned the house previously, had inherited the property from her parents. She owned the house on her own up until her death."

"Did she die in the house?" I ask, wondering if Irene has been the person haunting me this entire time. Something about that feels comforting to me—Irene doesn't sound evil or scary. I could continue to live in a house with her.

"Maybe, but I can't find a lot on her to know for sure. All I know is the house was sold by someone else after her recorded date of death."

"Hm."

Despite Stevie's earnest attempt at making this all sound more exciting than it is, it's pretty pedestrian. It's not exactly the unbelievable ghost story people really want—stories involving murders and people going missing and unexplainable details.

It seems like Stevie might be thinking the same thing. She shuffles through the papers in front of her like she's certain there's something in there.

"I'm going to be honest, I thought there might be more here for us," Stevie mumbles. But both she and Andrew let the camera run for a little bit longer, just in case—definitely holding out hope there might be something there.

I glance at Stevie and then look down at the papers in front of us. She's turned over what feels like every imaginable stone, even finding the original floor plans to the house.

"Bevere is a pretty unique surname, no?" I say. "Nothing much on her family?"

"Not in these archives," Stevie says. She sighs and then turns to Andrew, signaling for him to shut the camera off. "What a waste of time."

"I mean, maybe not. This is only what's made it into the newspapers, right? And the specific names mentioned?" I say, trying to be hopeful.

Stevie twists her lips and leans back in her chair."I don't know." She turns and looks at Andrew. "We might just need to work another segment in. Maybe we can share another story from the area or something. Or just make most of the episode about the house."

"There shouldn't be any shortage of things to film," I say. "I don't think I've had a single normal twenty-four hours since I moved in."

"And you really think it's a ghost?" Stevie asks and then reconsiders her question. "You've mentioned contractors. Have you tried any other avenues to explain the weird things going on there?"

"Not to speak on a woman's behalf, but I can't think of a single earthly explanation for what we saw at her house," Andrew interjects before I can answer.

I shrug in agreement. "He's right."

"It was just one thing, though. And it was so..." Stevie twirls her hand in the air as she searches for the words. "I don't know."

"I can't believe you've already forgotten. That shit was *weird*, dude. And scary."

"Just spend tomorrow at the house and see what happens," I offer, yet again in agreement with Andrew. "I'll let the house speak for itself."

Stevie lets out a breath through her nose. "I mean, fine. But I am a little nervous this episode might turn out to be less of a creepy ghost story and more of an *old house that just needs work*."

"That's not what your face said earlier, but okay," Andrew lightly argues, throwing a small smile in my direction. "But okay, if we go with Stevie's thinking—maybe we can try for an interesting LA history angle? I mean, it's LA. Even if a ghost isn't living in the house, something probably happened in the neighborhood. We introduce Lo, dedicate, like, five minutes to LA. Include the tour and then our footage from the house."

Stevie nods in thought, taking in his words. "It doesn't really take much to scare people with a ghost show. Showing off a dark house tends to be enough."

Andrew nods knowingly. "Exactly."

I look between the two of them. "My only contribution to this is that what you saw earlier is just the beginning."

Stevie smiles with amusement. "I'll take the challenge." She looks back over her shoulder at Andrew. "Should we see if your friend knows anything? Maybe the name Bevere will ring a bell for her."

"Yeah, let me check."

As Andrew digs his phone out of his pocket, I turn to Stevie. "Who's his friend? Another librarian?"

She's quiet for a beat, but her knowing smile sets me on edge. "You'll just have to meet her to understand, I think."

6

STEVIE

I've only met Andrew's friend, Valerie, a handful of times because she's hard to convince to leave the house. Or at least, that's about as much as Andrew's had to say about her.

After thanking Dr. Houston, Andrew gives Lo the directions to Valerie's house, and we get back in our van.

"Do you think she'll let us film?" I ask, glancing at the clock on the dashboard. It's already almost eight—the day is disappearing very quickly. "I'll let the idiots know we're going to be late on getting them, too."

"Yeah, she usually sleeps during the day, so I'm sure she just got up," Andrew says, only adding to the mystery that is Valerie. "I wonder if anything weird has happened while they've been there alone."

Tweedle-Dee and Tweedle-Dum are holding it down with the equipment back at the house, packing up for us, and then waiting until we can pick them up again. They're usually grateful for the break from us hovering over their shoulders, and I don't mind paying them to basically babysit our equipment—shit is expensive.

"I doubt it. One of them would've called us by now if something was going on."

"I don't know. They're so oblivious, I think a ghost could walk in front of them and they would have no idea."

I snort as I start up the car. "Fair enough," I say. "But I don't know. I don't think anything is really going on there."

"You're really giving up on Lo's house? Already?"

"I don't know, man. Gut feeling, I guess," I say and glance into the mirrors to pull out from my spot. "I don't think she's yanking us exactly, but this is pretty standard haunted house stuff, you know? This is shaping up to be pretty boring TV. People have seen this all a million times."

"The difference being that it's actually *real* this time." Andrew reaches forward to fiddle with the radio. We could afford a van, but not a very good one, so we still have a cassette player and FM radio, and that's about it. It makes our longer drives when we're shooting in places like San Francisco and New Mexico absolutely horrendous.

"This is all going to be for nothing. I shouldn't have let you talk me into this."

"You're such a drama queen. You'll thank me for this later, I'm sure," Andrew says. "And besides, it'd be nice to give actual ghost hunting a shot rather than just playing pretend."

"Are we still planning on setting up some stuff around the house?"

Andrew shrugs. "I don't think we need to, but we can."

"I'm really starting to think we'll need to. We're going to have to make up for the shitty storyline with at least one or two genuinely creepy things. People are going to watch because of Lo, so we need to go big."

"It'll be fine, boss," Andrew says, slapping down one of his massive hands onto my shoulders. "Not one single thing to worry about." When he sees the expression on my face, he puts his hands up defensively. "Or we can just scrap the whole episode and write it off as a learning lesson to not go somewhere to investigate just because we're asked. It's whatever."

"Thank you," I say, even though I know he's only saying it because I want to hear it, and flick on my turn signal to merge. It's late enough that the traffic isn't bad in Downtown proper. The Los Angeles freeways, however, are a different story.

But eventually, I pull in front of Valerie's place, an apartment complex tucked into a quiet street, and drive until I can find parking. We get out and walk up to the front gate, where Lo is standing. She's just on her phone, standing around, totally oblivious to my eyes on her. But she still somehow looks perfect. Her jeans fit every curve just right and the way her long blonde hair catches in the soft breeze is literally like something out of a movie. Seeing her like this—just out in the wild, separate from setting up to film—makes me realize she's exactly the kind of girl I'd see once at a bar and never forget.

By the time we approach her, I've made myself nervous to speak. I've gotten smoother over the years, but Lo has made me revert back into my sixteen-year-old self who's too scared to even look at her crush in the hall.

"Hey," she greets us as we walk up.

"Hey," Andrew says back. I can only nod coolly, my mouth dry.

Valerie comes down to meet us not much later and I'm relieved to have anything else to think about that isn't how being around Lo is making my palms slick with sweat.

"I like the purple," I say. Her hair had been dyed a vibrant green the last time I saw her, and then it was pumpkin-orange before that; I'm surprised by how healthy her hair looks despite the heavy dye.

"Oh, thanks. It felt right for October," she says. "Come on in."

The three of us follow Valerie through her open-air apartment complex. It's bigger than it looks from the outside—hallways extend on forever, and what feels like a million different staircases overlap with each other across the three stories.

She walks us up a nearby flight of stairs and pops open her front door using the weight of her shoulder. Her studio apartment is kept dim—not a single overhead light on. Everything is done up in deep purples and blues and blacks, from her rug to her sofa to the tapestries on the wall. It smells like weed and something else...like a musky perfume. The three monitors set up on her desk are the only thing that stands out as not matching the vibe of the rest of the place. From the floor, a tiny Yorkie yaps at us in greeting.

"Who's this handsome fella?" Lo asks and drops into a squat so she can offer her hand to him. An image of Lo meeting my dog pops into my head and I brush it off, refusing to go there.

"Locard," Valerie responds proudly. Her dog's head whips in her direction, tail wagging at the mention of his name.

"Unique."

"Named after the father of forensic science, Dr. Edmond Locard."

"Oh, wow," Lo says, and I can tell she's trying her best to find an appropriate answer. I fight off a smile.

"So, Andrew mentioned you guys have a question for me?"

"We're looking for something on a family who lived in the Eagle Rock area. There isn't much in the library archives, so we don't think anything went on, but we're trying to find some answers."

"Any particular reason?"

"There's a ghost in my house," Lo offers. "Allegedly."

Valerie's face lights up. "I love it—I grew up in a haunted house and I think it's what made me into who I am today, " Valerie says. Just like Dr. Houston, Valerie doesn't know the full truth about our show. As far as she knows, Andrew and I are both actual paranormal investigators.

"It's certainly building character," Lo says, and I wonder if she ever gets tired of hearing other people's opinions of her experience with her haunted house.

"I don't know if these guys have told you anything about me, but I'm an independent crime solver. On the side, at least. I work in freelance digital advertising as my actual job. But my passion is crime. I've become somewhat of an encyclopedia on things that have gone down in LA County basically since its inception."

To her left, standing deeper in the house and clearly more comfortable than Lo or me, Andrew nods. "That sounds like an exaggeration, but it's not."

"You're exactly who we might need," I say. "I don't know if we'll find anything, but the little detour is worth it since the library didn't give us much."

"I mean, libraries try their best, but sometimes things go missing. A name might be misspelled, or something wasn't able to be archived digitally. Or, my personal favorite—people change their names and become much harder to create a timeline on." Valerie sits down in her office chair. "Who are you looking for?"

"I'm going to start setting up to shoot if that's cool," Andrew says, and Valerie nods.

"The Bevere family," I say. "Irene Bevere owned the house at one point after inheriting it from her parents."

"And what's the timeline on this?"

"Irene inherited the house in the mid-1980s and then died in the 1990s."

Valerie takes in the information, nodding to herself. "Okay. I don't recognize the name, but that doesn't mean anything."

I sigh a little bit. If Valerie doesn't know anything, it's hopeless—there's no spinning this one. The best we can do is maybe get away with making up a story about the history of the house, but I don't know if Lo would feel comfortable with that. For being as entrenched in Hollywood as she is, she doesn't seem like a bullshitter. And that's coming from a professional one.

As Andrew fiddles with the camera, doing the best he can to set up a remotely interesting-looking shot—we've historically been able to do a lot with very little; it's part of the fun of learning the ropes with independent projects that have basically negative budget. Valerie clicks around on her computer. She's impressively fast despite having long, delicately decorated acrylic nails; I've never seen anyone type that quickly before, ever.

"Bevere..." Valerie mutters to herself. "Okay. I see what you mean about newspaper archives. There isn't much going on here for Irene. Or any Beveres in Los Angeles in the mid-twentieth century, for that matter, in case something odd went down with one of her relatives."

"Great," I grumble, unable to hide my annoyance. Andrew glances over my way, his way of telling me to stay cool. I'm trying not to get agitated, but this is all feeling like a wild goose chase and a terrible waste of a day. One weird thing happening at a house and a hot woman telling me it's a ghost doesn't actually mean anything. The further I get from the lights flickering, the less I believe it's anything more than just a random one-off issue with her electricity.

"Okay, this is interesting," Valerie says. I'm too deep into my own skepticism to experience any hope at her saying that. "The

Bevere family is linked to a *different* family tree—the Damoffs. It looks like Bevere was Irene's mother's maiden name."

I can't help but perk up—but only slightly—at that. People don't tend to change their names without reason. I take a step closer to Valerie. "Anything on the Damoffs?"

"Patience," she says, waving her hand over her shoulder with a dramatic flair. "Let the master work."

I keep my mouth shut as she types away on her computer, but I can't stand still on my feet. Valerie doesn't realize that her online search is the deciding factor on whether this whole thing—filming with Lo, exploring the possibility of actually investigating the paranormal, hoping that maybe all of this could bring us some exposure—has been worth it. But I very much know what's on the line.

Like with everything that ever happens with Paranormal America, my mind is racing at a million miles a minute. I've always struggled with never being able to do things calmly. I have Plan F ready before Plan A even starts, just in case everything falls apart.

But that's the field I've found myself in. In Hollywood, there's no time to be patient. No time to wait and see. When Andrew and I were waiting on next steps about the distribution of our show, I considered every bad possible outcome before I ever let myself believe something good might actually happen. Things move quickly. Until a contract has been signed, until things come together for an episode, there's nothing left to do but be ready to adapt. Scrap it all and start over from nothing.

I try not to be annoyed with Andrew for putting us in this position, but it's hard. It does feel a little bit like it was his fault for offering to investigate Lo's house in the first place. But I could've also nixed the idea more firmly. The appeal of investigating a celebrity's house had won out over my common sense of realizing what a stupid idea it was to go in with no story, no real plan.

"Okay, I'm not seeing anything," Valerie says with a sigh. Even she's having a hard time hiding her disappointment, and she's not even technically one of us. "Nothing on the Bevere family and nothing on the Damoffs. I don't think there's much of a story to your ghost. She's probably some spiteful old lady who died in her home and is upset she's still trapped between earth and the other side."

My lips turn up in a smile. One thing Andrew and I have been exposed to a lot over the course of filming our show is spirituality and people who are much stronger believers than us. I've had to get used to pushing down the scoffs and eye rolls that want to come out every time someone talks about ghosts like they're real. I can barely even handle astrology talk, and I've heard about it from pretty much every woman I've ever been on a date with.

"Maybe we can spin that somehow? Evil grandma?" Andrew asks, turning to me. Despite Andrew being by far the most levelheaded of the two of us, I'm the problem solver. And usually, the final say in terms of creative direction. Fortunately, Andrew makes up for his inability to construct a story on film with his many other skills.

"Not unless we get something about Irene specifically. It'll be hard to paint her as this, like, evil woman if we don't have an interesting story from her life to corroborate," I tell him. "And we don't even know if she died in the house, which is an added layer of difficulty."

The room is silent for long enough that I start to feel bad. I'm a blunt communicator, but I never mean for things to feel hopeless. I can tell when a silence is bad and also my fault.

I turn to Lo. "But you didn't buy the house from Irene, right?"

She shook her head. "No, Irene was the owner before the owners I bought it from."

"Maybe look into them," I say to Valerie, the buzz of momentum rising in my chest. There's nothing that I love more than the high of coming up with a solution to a problem. "Lo, what are their names?"

Lo chews on her lip in thought, and then her eyes suddenly light up. "The Davenports. Sunniva and Nico. But they only lived there for, like, four years, and they're both still alive."

"Maybe there's a reason they only lived there for four years," Andrew offers.

"Exactly," Valerie says, raising her eyebrows playfully. She turns back to her computer and begins typing. I glance over at her multiple screens and see that she's using a web browser I've never heard of. I don't bother questioning her methodology;

Valerie has the kind of air to her that makes me trust her technological skills way before I'd trust mine.

"Okay, interesting. Lo is right that they're both alive, but it looks like they might be internet personality types."

I let myself roll my eyes at that. "Yeah, them and everyone else in the city," I say.

"Well, they're not just any personalities." Valerie waves us over, and we crowd around her monitors. She's ended up on some webpage that can't possibly be for a real business based on the quality.

"What is a 'Spiritual Healer'?" I ask, trying to keep my face neutral. I'm already over it—there's no way to save this episode if this is the best we're going to get.

"It looks like a scam," Lo says honestly. "Believer or not in a higher power, I don't think this is legit."

"Wait, there's a video," Andrew says and reaches over Valerie's shoulder to press play.

Soft music plays out through Valerie's—admittedly very impressive—speaker system. The stars on the screen fade out, and a woman with straight black hair and no makeup smiles at us.

"Welcome," the woman says in an impossibly smooth and gentle voice. "My name is Sunniva. Now that you're here, I believe you were meant to find me. I understand the uncertainty and fear that you are feeling. In a world so large, so overwhelming, so isolating, we need to learn to rely on each other more than ever. Together, we can face what lies ahead. We can reclaim the parts of ourselves that have been lost. Join us in our journey to self-discovery and fulfillment. Become whole again."

The video fades out, her website URL replacing her face, and I blink at the screen, taking it all in.

"She's definitely a cult leader, right? Or part of a cult?" Lo asks, looking between all of us. "Asking in full seriousness. I've seen HBO documentaries with this same tone before, and the endings are never good."

"I don't know about a cult," I say, and I catch Lo's expression out of the corner of my eye. I shouldn't be turned on by a woman who looks borderline annoyed with me, but it's sexy when she does it. "That feels like a stretch. She's probably just a grifter."

"Maybe she's really a witch or something," Andrew offers. "If that's even the right term to use."

"Whatever the situation is, you guys have an easy in," Valerie says. "It looks like they have weekly 'self-connection' meetings somewhere in a neighborhood just outside of Riverside. And Stevie, you're going to love this—their next meeting is tomorrow night."

I think through the logistics. We'd have to drive out of town—almost definitely two hours one way at least from Lo's place—and meet up with a random group of people at a random address. It's a compelling story for sure—Sunniva alone is inherently a compelling story—but she doesn't seem like part of *our* story.

"I don't think I want to platform these people," I say. "And we've already hit a dead end once on this. I don't see a reason to put in all of that work just to show up and not get anything from them. Like, what connection would this random woman have to some ghost that's living in her former home?"

"I don't think you need to platform them, necessarily," Lo says. "But maybe they have some insight into why they moved. If they were experiencing similar things to what I've experienced, it could add an interesting angle. Or at least someone else who can vouch for the place being haunted. We just get their story and then retell it off-screen."

Andrew glances over at me, slight fear in his eyes. He knows I'm the show runner and the brains behind the operation. I don't mind input, but I also usually don't welcome it.

Lo, however, is right.

"It could be interesting," I admit. It's a big swing that might not offer any benefits at all, but a couple buying and selling a house that quickly for seemingly no reason at all—in this economy, and only to move less than one hundred miles away—is odd. "It's not like we have much else to go off of right now. We'll bring the camera just in case, but I'm not planning on filming them in any capacity."

Andrew presses his lips together. "Alright," he finally says. I've known him long enough to know he's only doing this because he's expected to go. He looks about as skeptical as I feel. Going so far out of our way to a place where we can't even shoot anything feels more like a waste of time than anything. But Lo has a point that they might have something interesting for us, and we need that right now.

"And after we crash their meeting—" I'm stopped by the sound of my phone ringing. I fish it out of my pocket. "The idiots are calling. Sorry. One second—let me make sure they didn't accidentally set the house on fire or something."

I step away from the group, which is only about six feet away because the apartment isn't very large, and accept the call. "What do you need?" I ask.

"You gotta get back here, dude. Some shit is going down," Tweedle-Dum says, breathing heavily into the phone like he just ran a marathon.

7

LO

Even though the website of the people who owned the home before me is undeniably fascinating, my gaze is pulled over toward Stevie. She's doing a good job of keeping her voice low enough that I can't really hear what's going on. But she looks stressed.

"Everything okay, Stevie?" I ask, mostly because the people who called her are presently at my house, and I want to make sure no one actually did burn it down. About one percent of me did it because I feel a schoolgirl crush setting in, even though Stevie is a strong personality and seems to have a compulsive need to do things like play devil's advocate.

Stevie gives me a nod of acknowledgement, telling me she'll give me an answer in a second. "We'll get back to you as soon as we can. Okay. Alright. Can you just hold on—alright. *Alright.* Jeez. We're coming."

She gets off the phone and looks at us. "They're saying something weird is going on at the house. I think we need to go."

"Did they say anything beyond that?" I think over the thousand possible things that the ghost—or whatever—living in my house could be doing to terrorize them. There's not one part of me that doesn't believe them.

"They didn't give any specifics. They actually sounded kind of shaken up." Stevie looks surprised by this, as if she wasn't there for what most people would consider a paranormal encounter just earlier today.

"We should get back. We can't afford to have them quit on us," Stevie says.

"Go back? Can't they Uber to the hotel from there?" Andrew asks.

"On whose dime?" Stevie asks. "We're going back."

I can see the hesitation written all over Andrew's face. He doesn't want to go back to the house.

"Isn't this supposed to be, like, your bread and butter?" I ask. "Going into an actively haunted house? Aren't you supposed to be jumping into action right now?"

"Not necessarily." Andrew takes on a somewhat defensive tone. "I'm just...not prepared for it right now. A ghost is still a ghost, even if you're an investigator."

Stevie shoots a glare in Andrew's direction that's so quick that it would've been easy to miss, and even easier to write off. But they've been having little moments like this all day to the point that I feel like I'm missing something rather than just making an assumption.

I look between them. "Personally, I would like to get back to the house just in case something bad is happening. It was not a cheap purchase."

Andrew nods. "For sure. Yeah," he says. He gathers the limited film equipment he brought with him. Locard, who'd been sleeping peacefully on the couch the entire time, jumped up from the sudden noise.

"Thank you for your help, Valerie," Stevie says, clapping a hand to her back. "This was really helpful."

"Good luck with your cult," she responds as Stevie, Andrew, and I head for the door.

"Not a cult," Stevie counters just before stepping back outside. When I shut the door behind us, Stevie sighs. "Alright, let's go retrieve the idiots."

My stomach is in knots just like it always is when I drive home. It's like getting the Sunday scaries over and over again, but it's every day and hits me every single time I try to go home. It's been months, and I still haven't gotten used to it. I'm surprised my hair hasn't started to fall out in clumps from the stress.

I park at the curb and wait for Stevie and Andrew before I head up to my front door. When I stare at my unassuming home through my window, everything seems normal enough—except for the two freshly-adult boys sitting on the front stoop.

I sigh a little bit and get out of the car. There's still no sign of Stevie and Andrew, but I also know the most efficient ways to get home. I wouldn't be surprised if they got caught up somewhere.

After shutting my driver's side door behind me, I approach Andrew and Stevie's interns. One of them is Sean and the other is Tanner, but they're identical so other than their shirt colors, it's impossible to tell which one is which. It doesn't help but Andrew and Stevie refer to them almost exclusively as *the idiots* or some variation of that.

"You guys okay?" I ask, feeling more like an older sister than someone who's supposed to be on-set with them.

"We're not going back in there," one of them says. He rubs his hands together, probably from the cold. It says a lot that they'd rather sit out in the chilly air—at least, as chilly as it gets in October in Los Angeles—than stay inside.

"What happened?" I asked.

"Dude—sorry," he says, stopping immediately, and I quickly realize that they view me more as their *mom* than even an older sister.

"It's fine," I say, refusing to let my ego be bruised. I'm used to people being assholes about my age in my industry, anyway, even though I'm not even thirty yet.

"I don't know what happened—"

"It's like we upset it or something," the other one cuts in.

"Yeah!" the first one says enthusiastically. "That's exactly it. It's like we upset it."

"It?"

"The ghost, but Sean is theorizing now it might be a demon."

I nearly let out a sigh of relief—finally, at least *one* of their names has a face. Not that it helps much since they're nearly identical; I'll have it straight until tomorrow, when I can no longer use *Sean is the one in the red shirt* as my visual cue.

But the relief is quickly replaced with a sinking feeling of dread. It had to have been bad if they're jumping to the word demon. "What exactly happened?"

As they're about to answer, the van pulls up to the curb. Stevie barely has it parked before she's hopping out of the car and rushing up the sidewalk toward us. "Yo, what are you two going on about?"

"She was asking us what happened," the one who isn't Sean—in the white shirt—says somewhat defensively.

"Sorry," Stevie says to me and then turns back to the boys. "You don't need to bother Lo about this stuff. Save it for me and Andrew—we'll get it sorted out."

"No, I want to hear about this," I say. The twins look at each other, fighting off obviously amused grins. I'm slowly piecing together that people on the *Paranormal America* crew don't talk back much to Stevie.

"She insists," Sean says, gesturing to me.

Stevie throws her hands up, quiet for a moment. "Alright. Go on."

Andrew lumbers down the path toward us. "Dude, you barely even parked that thing. Let me drive next time."

"Not a chance," Stevie says.

"What's going on?" Andrew asks as he tosses the van keys back to Stevie, who catches them easily with one hand.

Sean lets out a sigh of exasperation, telling me this happens often. "Jesus. Okay. We were inside. We'd packed everything up already—"

"Did you find the missing equipment?" Andrew asks.

"No, we couldn't find it anywhere," the twin in the white shirt says.

"Great," Stevie mutters.

I bit my tongue on making a comment about how their stuff was never coming back. I'm still yearning for the jacket that had gone mysteriously MIA from my dining room chair literally overnight a few weeks ago.

"*Anyway*," Sean continues. "We were inside just, like, on our phones or whatever when we heard someone opening the front door. We thought it was you guys at first, so we got up to go look but there was no one there, and the door was shut."

Stevie scowls at them. "That's what scared the shit out of you guys so bad we had to hurry home?"

"Well, wait. We were like, okay, that was weird, so we moved on. It was probably just a sound from inside the house. But then we started hearing what sounded like footsteps down the hall."

"Yeah, that happens," I say.

Sean gestures to me as if to say *See?* and then keeps talking. The fact that that isn't the end of his story makes me nervous. "That really started to put us on edge. But we were like, it's cool. We know it's a haunted house. We hung out for a little bit, and then a frame fell off the wall in the entryway. And then things that we'd packed up started falling off the table."

My heart thuds as I picture it. I haven't had anything to that level happen to me yet. I've had things go missing and heard weird sounds, but I haven't had anything happen that's so...*obvious*. Something so straight out of a horror movie.

"Things were falling? In front of you?"

"Yeah. Like, we saw them fall while we were sitting in the living room. And it was all for no reason. They were on the table one second and then not on the table another."

Unlike me, Stevie—of course—doesn't look moved. "You're absolutely sure?"

"I mean, you can go see for yourselves if you want. I'm sure it'll put on a show for you, too, if you're in the house long enough," the twin who isn't Sean says.

"I'll pass," Stevie says. "Maybe we can get some footage of the things that fell."

"I'm not going back in there," Sean says, shaking his head. He glances over at me like he's hoping I'll vouch for him.

"I don't want to go in either," Andrew says.

I glance between all of them. Maybe I would've been better off filming this place myself—for ghost hunters, they all seem a little too eager to get away from a haunted house. Other than Stevie, who keeps insisting there isn't a ghost at all.

Stevie stands there for a beat, thinking it over. "Alright. Let's just clear out for the night. We're doing one last investigative trip tomorrow, and then we'll shoot back here and wrap. Is everything packed up?"

"It was packed up, but now it's all over the floor," Sean says, giving her a well-practiced *I already said that, you fucking moron* eye roll. It'd never been so obvious how close in age he was to still being a teenager. It was admirable, but mostly because it was directed at Stevie.

"You guys are killing me." Stevie runs her hands through her hair. "Let's just get this stuff packed up. I'm starving and tired of thinking about whatever paranormal entity is terrorizing this house."

"Don't disrespect my ghost like that," I snap, and as Stevie whips her head in my direction, most likely ready to fight, I offer her a teasing smile. She backs down immediately.

Stevie turns to the twins. "Come on. Up and at 'em."

"I'm not going back in there. No fucking shot," Sean protests. His twin nods in agreement.

"You guys are being—"

"It's fine, I get it. I also spend as much time as I can avoiding this place. I can help instead of them," I offer.

Stevie looks at me and then at the twins, warning in her face. But she lets it go and pushes open the front door.

As soon as I step inside, that awful, sinking feeling that swallows me whole every single time I open my door greets me.

"God, this place really does give me the creeps," Andrew says, a visible shiver traveling over his body. He turns to me. "No offense."

I shake his comment off. "None taken. I have the same experience every time I open the door."

Stevie, a few steps ahead of us, turns into the living room and suddenly stops. "Jesus, dude."

"What?" I ask, taking quicker strides to see what she's seeing. The house might be haunted and the bane of my existence, but it's also *my* house.

I stop next to Stevie and don't even have to ask her what she's looking at. It's all laid out in front of us. The twins were right; things really were falling over the place. Equipment that I can only assume is expensive is on the floor, lights knocked over, papers all over the floor.

And it's not just things from filming, it's also my things that have been thrown everywhere. If I didn't know any better, I would've assumed a terrible wind storm had blown through and then just as quickly disappeared.

I gasp and walk over to my books that had been carefully lining my floor-to-ceiling shelves just earlier today. There weren't as many down here as there were in my bedroom, but the ones down here were my favorite decorative items to show off and my favorite conversation pieces. Most of them were signed copies or special editions of some kind.

"What the fuck?" I use my normal speaking volume, almost as if I'm talking to myself, but everyone in the room knows who I'm directing the question to.

I crouch down to pick up the books and put them back in their places. Stevie leans down beside me to help, surprising me.

But I don't make a comment about it because I can already tell Stevie is the kind of person who would get weird about me acknowledging a nice thing she's doing.

"These are cool," Stevie says as she looks at the books in her hands. We reach out for the same one and our hands brush. I jump, moving away before I can think too hard about how soft her skin is.

"Thanks. They're meant to be more decorative than anything but apparently *someone* here doesn't care about making sure the pages don't get bent," I say, making Stevie snort.

Our moment is interrupted by a voice of complete panic. "Guys, I think I want to get out of here. I have a really weird feeling—"

Just as Stevie turns, probably to tell Andrew to chill out, the lights flicker.

"Not this again," Stevie groans.

Even though it's the second time it's happened since they got here, it feels different this time. The flickers aren't in a pattern—they're sporadic, like we're leading into a power surge. After a few seconds, they cut out completely, leaving us in the dark. There's hardly any light at all coming through the windows now, too, so it's as dark as I've ever seen the house.

My heart jumps into my throat, panic immediately setting in. I want to sprint out of the house, ready to leave it all behind. But with the lights having changed on us so suddenly, it's taking time for my eyes to adjust.

Through the darkness, I can hear Andrew banging around to find a light switch. "The power is out," he says. "Fuck, dude. What the *fuck* is going on?" He's half-whimpering at this point, and I don't blame him for it.

"You okay?" Stevie asks, her voice low in the dark room. I don't dwell on how sexy it sounds or how much I like her voice when she's not calling everyone around her an idiot.

"Yeah," I lie, even though my palms are sweaty with genuine, blood-pumping fear. I've never experienced anything like this before. In all the time I've lived in this house, nothing has ever put me on edge this quickly. Normally, the ghost keeps things pretty inoffensive but this is starting to feel genuinely scary.

"I'll see if I can get the power back on. Stay here," Stevie says. I hear her put the books down on the shelf nearby, the living room still too dark to make out more than a hint of the objects in the room.

Just as my heart rate is finally about to level out, music suddenly blasts from down the hall. The noise is so loud and jarring that I physically jump. My hands find Stevie's arm in the dark, her muscles surprisingly toned to the touch.

It sounds like the ghost got to the record player I have in my room; it's playing through *Rumors* by Fleetwood Mac from where I'd initially left it off. "Never Going Back Again" had just taken the place of "Dreams."

"Oh my god," I breathe. The music is so loud I can't even hear my own voice.

"I'd never thought about this song as particularly scary until now," Stevie says, practically yelling, and a laugh rockets out of me, propelled by the anxiety I'm experiencing.

"What the fuck is going *on*, dude?" Andrew shouts from across the room. My eyes have adjusted enough to see him running his hands through his hair in a panic.

"I'm going to figure it out. It's fine. Everything is going to be totally fine," Stevie offers, raising her voice over the music.

"Don't go." I surprise myself with the words, but I'm not embarrassed—right now, at least. I probably will be tomorrow, or tonight when I'm lying in bed and just about to fall asleep. But the thought of being left here alone right now isn't sitting well with me. I want something—someone—sturdy to hang onto. To make me feel safe.

Stevie puts a supportive hand over mine, offering a squeeze. "Do you want to come? Which is worse—being left here alone or walking into the middle of it with me?"

I've never thought of myself as someone who's particularly dependent, but nearly paralyzing fear has a way of making even the most independent women give in.

Or maybe that's just me. And only because the opportunity is being offered by Stevie.

"I'll go with you," I say. Stevie steps closer to me and leans down to make sure she can hear me over the music that's still blaring through the house. I wouldn't be surprised if we're only a few minutes away from the police showing up from a noise complaint. As she steps closer, a wave of her cologne finds its way to me, and I have to stop myself from going weak in the knees. It turns out the only thing that might be stronger than fear is horniness.

I let go of her arm, and Stevie surprises me by finding my hand in the dark. Our palms are clammy but I don't mind.

"So we don't lose each other in the dark," Stevie says.

"Right," I reply as our fingers lace effortlessly together.

"We'll be back in a second," Stevie shouts. She fishes in her pocket and pulls out her phone, turning on the flashlight. In the split second I can see her phone, I'm greeted with her screensaver—a sweet photo of a black and white dog sitting on the floor in a patch of sun.

"Fuck this—I'm going outside," Andrew shouts back. True to his word, I hear Andrew turn the knob to the front door and swing it open. Even after he closes the door, his voice carries through the windows: "There is some seriously fucked up shit going on in there."

Stevie snorts. She holds her phone flashlight carefully to the ground ahead of us to make sure our walking path is clear. "Okay, ready?"

"I guess," I say, as Lindsey Buckingham keeps singing out the rest of his song. I know the album well enough to know it's about to switch over to "Don't Stop," which might be a little too upbeat for the situation at hand.

She gives my hand another supportive squeeze as we cut through the living room and head toward the front hallway. Instead of turning out the door like Andrew did, we head deeper into the house.

My house isn't very large—decent by LA standards, but that isn't saying much—but it's never felt so big before. I'm noticing every corner, every window, every place where something could jump out at us. I've always been a little scared of my house, but right now, I'm *really* scared of whatever is inside.

As we turn down the hallway to my bedroom, the music gets even louder and more overwhelming. My nerves aren't soothed by the sounds of what's one of my favorite albums of all time.

Stevie keeps up pace ahead of me as I start dragging my feet, uninterested in going any further. I glance back into the darkness, weighing my options. I could run outside and leave Stevie to figure this out on her own if I really wanted to. I'm sure Stevie wouldn't mind.

But that would require splitting up and I've seen enough Scooby-Doo—literally the only reference point I have on how to emotionally handle this—to know I'm probably better off sticking with someone than going anywhere alone.

My bedroom door is cracked, which opens up an even scarier possibility—maybe it's not a ghost but a living human being. Maybe there has been a simpler, albeit much more frightening, answer to my question of what the hell was going on.

I take a deep breath, half closing my eyes like I'm watching a movie instead of facing all of this in real life. Stevie is still keeping a steady pace ahead of me, cautiously pushing open the door all the way and then stepping into my room.

We hover near the doorframe for a second, Stevie's flashlight passing over different corners of the room. I hide behind her, gripping onto her arm.

I look at the room through partially shut eyes. The light glides smoothly over the surfaces of my room. Other than the music, nothing else is out of place or weird.

"Alright, let's get this turned off," Stevie shouts. She shakes her head like this whole thing has been an annoyance as opposed to the scariest thing that has ever happened to her. But then again, that's the whole point of her job. She's supposed to be able to handle this stuff; it's probably old news to her.

We cut across the bedroom, our steps quick this time instead of cautious, and Stevie points her flashlight at the record to figure out how to turn it off. When she finally manages to get it off, the silence that replaces Songbird is somehow even scarier than music unexpectedly blasting through the house.

"Weird," Stevie says.

"Very," I agree. "Can we get out of here now? I can hear my blood rushing in my ears, and it's making me uneasy."

Stevie chuckles. "Yeah, that's fine," she says. "We just need to pack up the rest of the stuff quickly."

"You can just leave it here overnight. It's fine," I say.

Even in the dark, I can see Stevie's amused smile. "Are you scared?"

"Of course I am!" I say. "What kind of question even is that?"

"But you've been living here for so long without a problem."

"This is...new for me."

Stevie waves it off. "It's fine. It's just something weird with the power.""And the stuff downstairs?"

"Not saying you should blame the idiots, but they are idiots. It's not like there's zero possibility it wasn't one of them. Or it could've been like, an earthquake or unsteady shelves or som ething.""I don't know. This feels really weird," I say. "Weirder than what I'm used to."

"You'll be alright," Stevie says. She lets go of my hand and I realize then that we'd been holding onto each other for that entire time. But as soon as she lets go, I want her to immediately come back.

"Where are you going?" I ask.

"Trying the lights again," she says. "Andrew's an idiot. For all we know, he managed to use the light switch wrong." She's quiet for a beat, the clicking sound of my light switch sounding out. "Okay, Andrew was right about that. But no big deal. I've been saying something is weird with your wiring, anyway."

"Right," I say, even though I'm not totally sure the answer is that simple. As much as I want to believe Stevie—really, *really* want to believe Stevie—it's becoming harder to think logically.

Stevie walks back over to me, standing only a few inches away from me. I can't really see her, but I can definitely feel her presence. Heat radiates off her body, and I'm desperate to touch her again and not out of fear this time.

The obvious then hits me like a punch to the gut. "Wait, if the power isn't on, how was the record player working?" The realization makes my stomach sink and my blood run cold.

I've been navigating the complexities of thinking there's a ghost in the house for months. And despite a million reasons to believe there's something weird going on, there's always a tiny part of me that refuses to believe it's really, actually happening. I'm not a full skeptic, but I'm cautious to go all-in on my ghost theory, and have been sitting at a steady ninety-percent certainty.

But this is the confirmation I'd needed. All of that time spent telling everyone about my haunted house, all of the stories and locking my bedroom door at night, and the weird feeling I get when I'm here—it all means something. The abnormal, crazy, unbelievable thing is exactly what's happening to me.

"Stevie, we need to get out of here," I say.

"It could just be some of the outlets in the house, random wiring—"

"*Stevie*," I plead, my voice carrying through the dark. I'm breathing like I just ran a mile.

She's quiet for a beat. "You really think something is going on?"

"I've never been so certain," I say. "I want to get out of here."

I wait for Stevie to argue or tell me that I'm being overdramatic. But instead, she just says in the softest voice I've heard from her, "Okay."

"Okay," I say, nearly letting out a sigh of relief.

Stevie directs her flashlight back toward my door, our lights joining together. We can make out most of the room now, but the limited light is making the world's scariest shadows bounce around us.

"My bedroom has always been the one room in the house where I wasn't scared, but not anymore," I admit.

"Do you want to go back with us?" Stevie asks.

"What do you mean?"

"Like, not stay here tonight?"

"Oh, no. It's fine," I say, my immediate impulse. And then after thinking about it a beat, I realize there's no way in hell I'm staying here alone tonight. "I'll just go to a hotel or something."

"That's where we're going, anyway," Stevie says. I'm quiet for a beat, and Stevie quickly manages to put together why. "Staying in hotels keeps us in the headspace of working, even if it's only a little bit of a drive away from our apartments. And it's tax deductible."

There's a part of me that wants to protest for some reason, but I know how stupid that is. I also can't think of anything worse than going somewhere by myself right now. I need people to decompress with after everything that's happened today.

And I also want just a little more time with Stevie.

"Okay," I say.

"Alright. Let's get you out of here." She nods her head toward the door and I follow her, our hands finding each other again. I'm squeezing tightly, using her like a human stress ball, but she doesn't seem to mind.

By the time the front door is in sight, I'm practically running to finally get outside.

"Dude, we thought you guys died," Andrew says as soon as we fly through the front door. Andrew and the twins have all settled into spots on my front stoop, sitting on their phones like nothing at all had just happened. "Can we get the hell out of here now, please?"

"Let's go," Stevie says, twirling her finger in the air to say *wrap it up*.

8

STEVIE

I can tell the guys are confused about why Lo is coming with us, but they have enough common sense not to ask questions.

"We'll come back for everything tomorrow," I say as I unlock the van. I walk around to the passenger side to open the door for Lo. She looks at me with some hesitation, like she can't tell if she's supposed to sit up there or not. "I'm not making you squeeze between all of them. You can sit up front."

"Enjoy the space," Andrew grumbles as he folds all 6'3" of himself into the backseat next to the twins. There's a decent amount of room because it's a van, but it's also mostly fitted for equipment rather than being able to sit comfortably.

Lo hops into the passenger side, and I shut the door before heading over to the driver's side. I start up the car and glance over at Lo to gauge her reaction. I can see in her face she's amused by the whole thing—the random stickers we've acquired at gas stations, the scratch marks, the random dents. It's our van and I love it, but that doesn't mean it's a good one.

I turn the radio on at a low volume. "Dinner?"

"Yes, please," one of the twins says.

"Diner food?"

"*Yes*," the other twin moans.

"Jesus. Keep your pants on," I say. "Alright, we'll go to our usual out here." I turn to Lo. "You don't mind breakfast food?"

She shakes her head. "That sounds delicious."

Even from Lo's house, I know the drive to the diner like the back of my hand. I've lived in LA long enough to have a decent mental map, even with how big the city is. It's not perfect, but there are certain places that are seared into my memory. I could find them no matter where I'm starting from, no matter how far I am, or how unfamiliar my surroundings are.

"God, I love this place," Andrew says.

"Thank god, I've had to pee so fucking bad," Tweedle-Dum says as I park. The car isn't even off by the time he's throwing open the side door and sprinting up to the entrance.

I get out of the car and meet Lo on the sidewalk. She looks up at the restaurant—a classic, retro-style diner with a neon green sign. It's open twenty-four hours, and the food is reliably good. It's one of my favorite places on earth. I can't help but admire the way the glow from inside makes her hair look golden even in the dark.

"You been here before?"

"No, I haven't," Lo says. She wraps her arms around herself to brace against the chilly breeze that sweeps over us. "It's cute, though."

I place a hand on Lo's lower back to lead her in the right direction. When we open the front door and step inside Anita, the waitress who I've seen a million times, smiles. It's quiet inside just like it always is in the later evening. It's too far from any of the major bars out here for people to want to wander to, so it's usually just the regulars or people craving a sober late-night meal. "Oh, you guys again. Welcome back," she says warmly. "I thought you were out of town for a shoot this week."

"No, ma'am. Change of plans," I say.

"And you've brought someone new along," she says, nodding to Lo. Anita looks up at me, playfully raising her light gray eyebrows. "She's very pretty."

"She is," I say. "She's also hungry, like the rest of us are."

"Coming right up," she says and waves us down the aisle of booths. We settle into one of the larger ones, tucked into a back corner near the windows. The twins—both of them back after sprinting to the bathroom, continuing to feed into the belief that they do actually share one brain cell—slide into the booth with Andrew. I sit down after and Lo sits down next to me, taking the seat at the end.

"I didn't realize how hungry I was until I smelled the food here," Lo says. When Anita places a menu in front of her, Lo smiles. "Thank you."

"Of course, sweetie pie," Anita says with a grin. "I'll come back in a few. I'm assuming you're all just going to want your regulars, but I'll let the new girl have a minute."

Just as Anita predicted, the only person looking at the menu is Lo. The rest of us take a moment to breathe for the first time in what feels like ages.

"That was nuts," Andrew says. "I *never* want to do that again."

"Was it really that bad compared to what you guys are used to?" Lo asks.

I try to think of a way to diplomatically answer her question. It *is* bad compared to what we're used to because normally, the places we go aren't actually haunted. But I can't exactly tell her that. "Yeah, your house is pretty active," I say. "There's a lot more going on there than I thought when we first agreed to this."

"Are you looking forward to visiting the cult compound tomorrow?" Andrew asks. "That might give us some answers."

"Not a cult compound," I say, rolling my eyes. "I don't know. I can't figure out how to feel about it. I don't know if it's going to actually lead to anything."

"I guess we'll see," Lo says.

"Do we really need an explanation as to what the deal is with the ghost if we know there's a ghost?" Tweedle-Dee asks with a shrug. "Like, someone died in the house at some point. A ghost is there now. End of story."

"It's TV, it needs to be more exciting than that," I say.

Anita swings by again to get our orders down. Andrew, the twins, and I order an impressive amount of food—tax deductible again—and then turn to look at Lo.

"I'll just do the regular breakfast meal," she says. "Bacon. But chocolate chips in the pancakes, please."

"You got it, baby," Anita says and collects our menus.

I take a sip of the diner coffee that I can't resist, even when it's late. Time flew at Lo's, and none of us seem particularly motivated to rush out of here, so it'll be a while until we're at the hotel for the night.

"Lo, I'd ask you how your first ghost hunting experience was, but I guess you've already been an expert," Andrew says as he takes a sip of his own coffee.

She smiles. Now that the adrenaline is gone, she looks sleepy more than anything. It's cute the way her eyes are drooping just the tiniest bit. I fight off the urge to offer to tuck her into bed. "That was definitely more exciting than I'd been anticipating. I was honestly a little worried you guys were going to come and nothing was going to happen."

Andrew shook his head. "No. It's almost like the ghost was pissed because we were there."

Lo nods, deep in thought. "Yeah, honestly. You're right. I don't think I've ever had so many major things happen consecutively like that before."

"Are you going back there tonight?" one of the twins asks.

"No way." She shakes her head. "I might live in a haunted house, but I know my limits. I don't think it's going to, like, kill me or anything, but that doesn't seem like a game I want to play."

"I don't blame you. I'd sell the house if I were you," the other twin says.

Lo looks between them. "I'm so sorry. I only know one of your names. You're Sean, right?" she says, and Sean—Twee-dle-Dee—nods. "Who are you?"

"Tanner."

"Thank you," Lo says, and I can see visible relief on her face. The moment is so sweet that it makes me think that *maybe* I could lighten up on the boys a little bit. They might be idiots, but they're our idiots.

Anita brings the food over a minute later and my stomach growls at the sight. The day has been so busy that we haven't eaten anything since early this morning.

"I feel like today has been a lifetime," Lo admits. She douses her pancakes in syrup and passes it off to Andrew, who pours it over his French toast.

"It's been a really, really long day," Andrew agrees. "I feel bad, Xavier has been trying to get a hold of me all day, but I haven't known what to say to him. I'll have to call him when we get back to the hotel."

"Xavier is Andrew's boyfriend," I explain quietly to Lo. It's been so long since we've had anyone new in the mix that I forget that she doesn't know everything.

"Sort of boyfriend. He's twelve years older than me and it's not serious. At least, right now," Andrew says. "We'll see how things go."

Lo smiles. “It’s nice to talk about things that aren’t the ghost in the house. I kind of forgot there’s a whole world out there.”

“Speaking of, is your friend single?” Tanner asks.

“She is, but she’s too old for you,” she answers. She looks at Tanner for a beat. “And I am, too.”

He plays it off, but I can see the disappointment in his face. I snort out a laugh, covering up the fact that I’m relieved to hear there’s no one else in the picture.

After eating so much it leaves all of us moaning and gripping our stomachs, we head back to the van.

“Where do you guys usually stay when you’re in a hotel out this way?” Lo asks.

“*Usually stay* is generous. We just started making enough money to do things like this. We’ve only done a hotel stay in LA County twice before. When we were working on our first season, we had to all stay in one room together because we had, like, ten dollars between all of us. We were shooting around Granada Hills, and none of us wanted to drive back home after a fourteen-hour production day.”“I get that,” Lo says.

“But we picked a place kind of near you to make things easy,” I say. “LA tends to be the most expensive of the places we stay. When we were shooting in Utah last year, we stayed at a hotel for I don’t think more than seventy bucks a night.”

“Yeah, and it was scarier than the haunted place we were filming in,” Andrew interjects from the backseat.

“It’s part of the fun,” I say, waving off the comment. I pull the van away from the curb and head off toward the hotel. It’s only a ten-minute drive, but it feels like a lifetime. After bouncing between places so much today, I'm ready to stay put somewhere for a while.

Eventually, we make it to the hotel. I pull into a parking spot, and we all jump out of the car. As we grab our bags from the back, I look at Lo and realize she's the only one without anything. "Shit. We didn't pack you a bag."

"That's okay. I wanted to get out of there so badly that I don't mind. I'll figure it out," Lo says. "All that matters is that hotels have free shampoo and toothbrushes. I'll rewear clothes until tomorrow morning if I have to. The bigger issue, though, is that I don't have my wallet."

"Oh, shit," I say. "I guess it's a good thing that we offered to put your meal on our business card, then."

"Ha-ha," she says, rolling her eyes, as we start a slow walk up to the hotel entrance. "But no, genuinely. I am glad. This does, however, make things weird. I can sleep in the car if I need to. Or I guess Uber back to my house."

"I'm not letting you go back there alone tonight, you're not going to sleep," I say. "We'll just put this on the card, too. It's fine. There's always extra money in the budget for a reason."

"I'll Venmo you."

"We can figure it out," I say. I'm not going to say it out loud because I know Lo will protest, but I'm not interested in taking her money from her.

We go inside, and it takes me walking up to the desk for the receptionist to acknowledge that we're there. "Checking in?"

she asks. Her tone of voice suggested she'd rather be anywhere but here.

"Yes," I say, unaffected. "I have three rooms, all under Anderson. And I'd like to add a fourth."

"We're all booked out for the night," she says. Then, as if remembering she works a customer service role, she turns to me and shrugs. "Sorry."

"I can just head out, it's fine," Lo says. "I don't have anything with me, anyway."

"No, no. It's cool." I turn back to the receptionist. "Can we get extra keys for the double room, please?"

She offers me the most exhausted, pained expression a person could possibly make. "Yeah, okay," she says.

"Stevie, it's really fine–"

"No, I insist. I'd rather you be here than back there tonight. You deserve a good night of sleep."

"But it's going to be putting one of you out. I don't want to be an inconvenience."

"It's really fine. We've all been working in the industry to know that this is how it goes sometimes. And our show sends us all over the map—LA is one of our more populous destinations. The hotels are a lot nicer."

"It's true," Andrew says from behind me, not looking up from his phone. I hadn't even realized he'd been listening.

I look back at the receptionist who's completely unmoved by the entire conversation unfolding in front of her. "Two keys?"

"Please," I say. "And a toothbrush and toothpaste."

The receptionist doesn't even try to fight off her sigh. "Fine," she says. She heads into the back office and drops a travel-sized toothpaste and a plastic toothbrush into my hand. "Okay, that's everything."

I fight off a smile. Speaking for myself as an asshole, I rarely mind when someone else. I don't like dumb questions or dealing with morons, but I know how to handle someone everyone thinks is unnecessarily mean. Working in direct service at a hotel would definitely do that to a person.

"Thank you," I say. I pick up the hotel keys and hand them off accordingly—the twins share a room, and then Andrew and I get our own because we're usually up all night working anyway and like the quiet.

"What's your plan?" Andrew asks, not-so-subtly looking between me and Lo.

"We'll just take the room that has separate beds. It'll be fine," I say and then turn to Lo. "As long as you don't mind, I'll be looking over footage and wrapping up some stuff from the last episode."

"I'll take what I can get," Lo says.

We head to the elevators to get to the third floor, where our rooms are all only a few doors away from each other. I peek into each one until I find the double-bed room that I booked for the twins. But after pushing open each door, I quickly realize that they didn't give us one.

"I think they made a mistake with the booking," I say.

"Or you made a mistake while booking." Andrew takes the key from the closest room out of my hand. "Not my problem. Have fun, you crazy kids."

My cheeks light up with heat, and I turn my face, hoping that Lo can't see. Even though it's obvious what Andrew is implying and I want Lo to know that's absolutely *not* what's going on here, it'll make things weird if I bring it up first.

"See you tomorrow, boss," the twins say. Tanner tosses one last glance in Lo's direction, and I shoot a glare in his direction, reminding him to keep his eyes to himself.

Lo and I are then left alone in the completely silent hallway. Despite the receptionist telling us the hotel was completely booked out, the lack of seemingly anyone else in the building suggests a different story.

"I didn't do this intentionally," I blurt out. Any ounce of coolness Lo might've thought I had just disappeared completely with that one sentence, I'm sure of it. "I really did book a double room. I always do it for the twins."

"I believe you, it's okay," Lo says in the same kind, even tone she's been using the entire day. She's impossibly gentle and warm, like the human embodiment of sunshine. I'm left with no other option but to want to bask in it for as long as she'll let me.

"She even acted like she knew what I was talking about when I asked for keys to the double room." I shake my head and readjust my backpack—I've learned the value of packing light over the years—on my shoulders. "I'm sorry. I can sleep on the floor or something."

"It's fine, they usually have king beds in single rooms like that. We'll be so far apart that I'll barely even know you're there."

It takes everything in me not to say *Speak for yourself.*

The entire time we're walking back to our hotel room, I have to concentrate on my breathing. I press the card against the reader and wait for the light to turn green, my hands sweating unnecessarily the entire time. I've never felt more like a bumbling idiot in my life. It's like I'm in high school, taking the prom queen home after the dance to have sex for the first time, except I was never on any prom queen's radar when I was in school. The high school film bro thing didn't exactly play out well in my suburb growing up.

The room is about as straight-forward as any chain hotel room—a bathroom, a TV, a small closet. The giant bed. As soon as I see it, I'm certain I've made a huge mistake.

"I can just sleep in the car, honestly. It's not a big deal," I offer.

"It's fine, I promise," Lo says, but I can see her eyes also fixed on the bed. Sleeping in the same room—in the same *bed*—is one thing in theory, but a totally different thing in practice.

Both of us hover by the door. I'm not sure I'm brave enough to make the first move and pretend this is normal and like we didn't just meet each other for the first time less than twelve hours ago.

"I'm serious about sleeping on the floor. There's a blanket in the closet. Or the chair seems comfortable," I offer, fighting off the swirling, out-of-body feeling sitting in my chest. It turns out the only thing that can get my heart rate to skyrocket more than a potential ghost encounter is being left alone in a hotel room with a hot woman.

Or I shouldn't even say any hot woman—Lo, in particular. Being here alone with her is doing something weird to my confidence. The practiced LA-cool persona I've perfected over the years completely crumbles, and all I'm left with are memories of all of the times I've been uncool.

This is a nightmare.

"You should get a good night of sleep," Lo says. "Or even just a nap, if you're planning on working most of the night anyway. I'm exhausted because we're already, like, two hours past my usual bedtime so I'll knock out and you won't hear from me again until checkout tomorrow."

"It's fitting you're not a night owl," I say.

Lo laughs, and the tension in the room finally eases. I slowly inch my way into the room, dropping my bag down on the desk and then going over to the bed. "What do you mean it's fitting?"

"You read and listen to Fleetwood Mac on vinyl. I'm sure you also mostly drink tea and like to take regular walks to make sure you get enough sun in for the day."

Lo's jaw goes slack, and I can see her trying to think up a response. She then folds her arms across her chest. "Okay, weirdly perceptive. I don't think I like that, actually."

"It's part of reality TV. You have to be able to figure people out." I lift the edge of the mattress as I'm talking and look underneath, inspecting the sheets carefully.

"Is that most of your background? Even before you started Paranormal America?" Lo asks and then pauses. "What are you doing?"

"Bedbugs," I explain and then put the mattress down when I don't see anything. "We travel too much to take risks like that. I heard you can check for them this way at hotels."

"Is that actually effective?"

I shrug. "Honestly, I have no idea. But it makes me feel better." I kick off my shoes and push them up against a wall near the front door so they're out of the way. "And yeah, pretty much all unscripted stuff. It's not exactly what I had in mind for myself, but it's...fun, I guess. There's always work."

"What did you want to do instead?" Lo asks. Her cheeks flush. "Sorry, I didn't mean for this to turn into twenty questions again. I don't know why I keep grilling you."

"No, it's okay. I guess I wouldn't expect you to look into my background beyond the ghost stuff," I say. "If it makes you feel any better, I didn't know who you were at first. Andrew had to fill me in."

"Andrew's a fan?"

"Of course, he's seen all one million seasons."

"He's being pretty cool about it," Lo says. She wanders around the room, brushing her hand over the comforter in thought. "Not to sound like a cliche, but it has been nice to feel normal around you guys. So many years of my life were tangled up in one show and one character. It's nice to be something else, even if it's that I'm the girl who lives in a haunted house."

"Allegedly," I say with a half-smile, teasing her.

She looks up at me with a matching smile on her lips. "*Allegedly,*" she says. "I don't think I've met another person who likes to play devil's advocate as much as you do."

I throw my head back with a laugh. "What's that supposed to mean?"

"You're so skeptical of everything. I feel like I could tell you my shirt is white and you'd tell me it's actually yellow just on principle."

I sit down in the office chair next to the desk and think over her words. "Yeah, fair enough."

"Personally, I don't know what else you could possibly need to prove that my house is haunted. It seems pretty evident to me."

"Yeah, I don't know. I guess it's just so...extreme to me. Like, *ghosts*? Really?"

"A paranormal investigator who doesn't believe in ghosts—I didn't expect that when I reached out to you guys."

I realize my mistake as soon as she says that. I'd forgotten that my real opinions don't matter right now—I have to be *the* ghost girl. Number one believer in the paranormal and unexplainable.

"Oh, yeah, I just mean I've seen so much. It takes a lot for me to be truly convinced. I don't take it lightly."

"Right," Lo says, and I can't tell if she's starting to see the cracks in my story or not. I've never been a particularly convincing liar—it's easier to stretch the truth and avoid answering as much as I can. "So, what was it that you wanted to do if not reality TV? You never answered my question."

"Film," I say simply, "like just about everyone else here. I got my start as a kid making dumb movies in my backyard. And then I became more serious in middle school and *very* serious in high school. I did a couple of short films and really tried, but...I don't know. You just end up where the money is sometimes."

"Yeah, I actually really feel that," Lo says. She sits on the very edge of the bed—it feels too weird to think of it as *our bed*—and sighs a little bit. "I know the show I was on basically bought me the house, but it's complicated. Too many years of auditions that went nowhere have kept me grateful, though. I know there are people out there who wish they had what I had."

"It's the price of loving something, I guess. I can't see myself doing anything else, even when the exact job I have isn't my first choice."

"Do you not like the show?" Lo asks.

"That's the first time anyone's ever asked me that." I pick at the hem of my shirt in thought, turning myself back and forth in my chair. "I don't know. I actually think I might really love it, but I feel weird admitting it. I get to travel. I have a lot of creative control. We're a small crew with a very small budget, which makes things feel more...grassroots, I guess. It's about as barebones as something can be on screen. Feels like I'm back in short films again, where it all started or whatever."

Lo's face softens, and I have to look away, embarrassed to have been so vulnerable. Andrew and the twins aren't particularly sentimental, so I'm not sentimental with them. We don't talk about hopes and dreams or if we like what we do. We don't talk about anything related to feelings, really, other than being annoyed or tired. It's weird working that muscle in myself again and remembering that I have the capacity to be gentle.

"I think you could do well in horror. With all of the ghost talk and having to make things scary while telling a story," Lo says and leans her weight back onto her arms.

Forgetting she's right there, my eyes trail over her frame. It's hard, if not impossible, to pull my eyes away from the crease where her thighs meet her hips. I want to put my hands on her waist, run my hands under her shirt...

I force myself to look away. I've been on my best behavior all day, doing everything I can to not get distracted by Lo. But now that we're alone and there's no more work to focus on, I find myself getting wrapped up in her. There's something about the way her hair falls over her shoulders, her sweet smile, the gentle but firm way she communicates. Her confidence, her certainty, are so fucking sexy. I've never liked a woman putting me in my place—never *let* a woman put me in my place—before now. And I'm really liking it.

"Yeah, I'll consider," I say, the most half-assed, distracted answer I've ever given to a question. I feel like a student who just got called on while daydreaming.

Lo is either genuinely a great actress, or she can't tell how much I'm fighting for my life right now. It's taking every cell in me not to ask her if I can kiss her. "I just can't believe you didn't film any of the stuff from earlier," she says.

I bring my eyes back to her face, which doesn't help much with fighting off my growing desire for her. "It'll be fine. I'm sure we'll see just as much tomorrow."

She groans. "I don't like the sound of that."

"I mean, you don't have to be there for it. We've gotten all of the filming we need out of you," I say. "We just need your house now."

"I feel like I should be there."

"You really don't have to be," I say. If anything, it's better if she's not there so we can blow through filming and set up props or fake spooky scenarios if we need to keep the episode interesting. But I can't exactly tell her that.

"I don't have much of an option. It's my house; I'm going to just keep living here. No matter what happens tomorrow, I'm...stuck. I'll just have to make it work. And it's not like I have anything better to do than spend time in my house, anyway, even if I'm not on camera."

"It'll be alright." As soon as I say it, I know it's lame. Lo is clearly upset; telling her it'll be alright is just an empty promise.

"Maybe we'll figure out it's all fine, and it really is just like a weird wiring issue or something. All hope is not yet lost."

"Are you able to get rid of the ghost for me?" she asks.

My lips turn up in a smile. "That's not really our specialty."

"And to think my biggest concern yesterday was that I was going to look nuts for thinking there was a ghost in my house. Now, I'm like, so I have to *sell* my place? Keep coexisting with some kind of paranormal entity that's getting increasingly annoyed with me?" She throws herself down onto the bed, her sun-kissed blonde hair falling over the side. She turns to look at me, and I almost have to look away. It's hard to believe someone can really be *that* naturally beautiful. "Do you really think there's a chance it's not a ghost?"

"I think there's always a chance it's not a ghost. But we'll see how tomorrow goes," I say. All day, I've been tossing around ideas in my head about what to do to keep this episode interesting—and believable. Even with the weird things going on in the house, everyone is going to poke holes in it. People love to watch a ghost show just to poke holes in it; I pride myself on being as solid as possible. I want it to be so good that I can convince the skeptics of the world—people like myself—that we really did have a ghostly encounter.

It helps to play things up on camera, setting up practical effects and faking certain scenes to really sell people. But with Lo there, I'm not sure there's going to be a way to do that. We'll just have to hope we can cut things together to make it compelling, even without the record player incident caught on camera.

I could kill Andrew for getting us into this mess. I'm starting to not regret it as a reason to be introduced to Lo, but I am regretting everything else about it. This episode has been a complete mess. And even as someone who can crush several energy drinks in one day and survive off no sleep like any good member of production—I want my TV to be solid. I don't want to make an episode I don't feel good about.

Lo turns her head and looks up at the ceiling. "I'm scared for tomorrow."

"The, like, spiritual group or whatever? It'll be fine."

"No, I have a really bad feeling about the house. Things have always happened in it, but it seems like it's getting exponentially worse. I've never felt the need to spend a night away from it; I'm worried about what'll happen when we go back."

Even I know when it's not the right time to make a joke. "We'll be there to look out for you. Nothing bad is going to happen."

She sits up again and looks at me. Her hair is tousled now from the sheets, and all I want to do is run my fingers through it. And the look on her face is killing me—I've never viewed myself as a protector type, but I know I'd do anything to make Lo feel safe.

"At least it'll be a good episode. And you have video proof now backing up your claims," I say, trying to ease some of the heavy air that's filled the room. I can tell Lo isn't feeling one-hundred; it's written all over her face and the way she's picking at the material of the comforter.

"You really think it'll be a good episode?"

"Yeah," I lie. It's not that I think it'll be a *bad* episode, but I don't know if it'll be a complete slam dunk. Shows that are at least a little scripted—even reality shows—tend to play out better than shooting raw footage and hoping for a story. I like the security blanket of knowing what's going to happen next. But I can't exactly tell Lo that without blowing everything up. "I can tell you're an actress."

Lo's brows furrow for just a second. "Meaning?"

"You're good on camera. Very well-spoken. I think no matter what happens, people will like seeing you on camera and hearing you talk about what's been going on in your house. It'll end up all being worth it, even if the episode is missing some bigger scary moments or whatever."

Lo's lips turn up in an amused smile. "Careful, saying too many nice things, Stevie, I might start thinking you have a soft spot for me," she teases.

The way she says my name makes me so tongue-tied that I can't think of a response, and I end up letting out an awkward chuckle instead.

"Is it okay if I shower?" Lo asks.

"Yeah, of course." I hope my voice is more level and cooler to her than it sounds to me. My face lights up hot at the idea of Lo being naked in my general vicinity.

"Also...do you have any clothes?" she asks sheepishly. "I'm really sorry."

"Oh. Yeah." I clear my throat. "Of course," I reach for my backpack and pull out the pajamas that I was going to wear tonight.

I hand off my clothes to Lo, and she looks at me. Neither one of us lets go of the clothes. "Am I asking too much of you? It's okay, you can tell me. You've already been so nice, I don't want to risk overstepping."

"No, I promise—it's really fine. You should be comfortable. I might not even sleep much tonight since I'll be working on stuff anyway. I'll just sleep in the shirt I'm wearing tomorrow, it's not a big deal."

"But you're supposed to film in that."

"People tend to like their paranormal investigators a certain amount of disheveled. It adds to the appeal."

"Good point," she says, and then finally takes the clothes from me. "Thanks."

"Yeah, of course."

I have to pull my eyes away from her as she heads away from me and toward the bathroom.

9

LO

I did not have showering with Stevie only a wall away from me on my list of things that were going to happen today.

It's literally the only thing that I can think about as I'm brushing my teeth and then turning on the water—an impressive feat considering I'm currently taking shelter from the ghost in my house.

But it's hard *not* to think about it. Realistically, it shouldn't feel any different than showering at a friend's house. I've done it hundreds of times before. And I'd navigated communal showers when I was in college, which should've felt like the least private, least intimate showering experience a person could have.

But instead, all I can think about is how Stevie is right there. Just sitting in her all black with her perfectly messy hair and flashes of tattoos when she lifts her arms. I'm about to be naked so close to her, and even if she's not thinking about it, I definitely am.

And that's exactly *why* I can't be normal about it. Unlike all of the other times I've used someone else's shower, I find

Stevie hot. Really hot. Sexy in a disheveled, confusing kind of way that I'd never really liked in anyone else before. She's blunt but also deeply kind underneath her hard-to-hear exterior. I love watching the way she interacts with people, the kindness in her conversations with the librarian and our waitress.

I drop my clothes to the floor and look at the pajamas she'd offered me for the night. It feels so intimate to be wearing her clothes, but I guess there are few things more intimate than sharing a room—sharing a *bed*—so clothes feel pretty minor in comparison.

I step into the shower and let the hot water run over me. I take a deep breath and force my body to relax. This is the first shower I've taken somewhere that isn't my house since I bought it, and it's strange to not hear anything, to not be hyperaware.

Instead of thinking about the various horror movie fates that could befall me—a la *Psycho* mostly—I'm thinking about Stevie. And while she's not a threat to me or putting me on edge, she's certainly not helping with keeping my heart rate level.

I take my time rinsing my hair and my body, enjoying the peace. Showers can be so vulnerable, especially when I have to close my eyes or turn my back, and it's nice to finally not feel like prey being hunted.

After taking as much time as feels appropriate in the shower, I turn off the water and pat my skin dry. I wish I'd had the foresight to bring anything at all with me—I miss my moisturizer—but it hadn't exactly been top of mind. There'd been about a million other things to worry about instead.

I towel off my hair and pull Stevie's t-shirt over my head. It's oversized and deliciously soft. There's a faint scent of detergent and something else, a faint musky cologne, maybe, that lingers in the fabric. It's annoyingly comforting, somehow smelling and feeling like home—an unhaunted, comforting one—even though we'd met just hours ago.

I step out of the bathroom and shiver from the temperature change. A cloud of moisture follows behind me like I just stepped out of a sauna, telling me I was in there for way longer than I thought.

"How was it?" Stevie asks. She's sitting in the office chair with her laptop on the desk in front of her. She has an attached monitor playing video clips. I can tell it's footage from earlier today; I recognize my front stoop, my living room. It's weird seeing it in b-roll form, like I'm seeing my house for the first time truly through someone else's eyes. It looks like a set I would work on more than my home.

"It was nice," I say and sit down on the edge of the bed. I towel off the ends of my hair. "Very needed."

"I bet." She glances back at her computer screen. "Nice outfit. I never pictured you as a boxers kind of girl."

"Yeah, you like it?" I ask, teasing. A tiny signal in the back of my mind sounds off: She's flirting with me. And even if she isn't, it's cute that she's suddenly lost the ability to make eye contact with me. "Thanks, I really love the..." I pull the shirt away from my chest and look down to read the front. There's an abstract illustration that looks delicately hand-drawn and then printed, along with a name. "Wyatt County Jaguars."

Her cheeks light up, but she keeps her eyes locked on the screen in front of her. "My high school. I didn't think anyone would see the clothes I was sleeping in."

As stupid as I know it is, I like that she didn't pack with bringing a girl back to her hotel in mind. I know how producers—and people in Hollywood in general—can be. It's not like I can blame her since she's single, but I like knowing there's no one in LA she's inviting back to her hotels. "Cute. California?"

"Arizona."

"I like it. A new look for me," I say. "I didn't realize you were from Arizona."

She arches a dark brow at me. "Because I seem like such a California girl?"

"You're so..." I wave my hand around, trying to find the word. "Intense. Arizona seems sunnier than that. Friendlier."

Stevie bites back a smile. "It has a lot of interesting history. The desert, ghost towns."

"Aliens," I offer, and she playfully rolls her eyes.

"I know a lot of people like the stories from the, like, old Victorian mansions, but I've always preferred the ones connected to nature. There's a lot there that we don't know. I'm hoping to go bigger with my show—less time in houses and more time filming in cooler destinations. Bayous, deserts, mountains. That kind of thing."

"Did you have any, like, encounters back home? Is that what inspired you to start ghost hunting?"

"Nothing specific happened to me, but I heard a lot of the stories growing up." Stevie turns away from her computer and finally looks at me instead. For her sake, I pretend I don't see her eyes flick over my body.

I subtly adjust my posture in response, surprised by how intensely I'm craving her approval right now. I wouldn't say I feel particularly sexy—Stevie is right that oversized boxers are not really my thing—but being here alone with her is making something come alive in me that hasn't in a long time. Even flirting with someone at a bar doesn't carry this kind of pull. We're so close, forced together into such a small space. It's hard not to at least consider what it might feel like to kiss her soft, full lips.

"Stories?" The word slips out of my mouth, the best I can come up with when the majority of my brainpower is focusing on how it would feel to have Stevie between my thighs.

"Yeah, you know. Weird encounters. My grandparents live in one of those desert towns with, like, five hundred people. It seems like everyone there has a story about hearing a random voice when no one's around or seeing a figure."

With Stevie sharing details about her family, it suddenly feels wildly inappropriate to be this horny. I take a deep breath, forcing myself to be normal about the way she keeps absent-mindedly rubbing her bicep under her shirt, showing off her tattoos.

"That's really cool," I say, and I mean it even though to my ears, it sounds like the kind of thing a man who's desperately trying to get laid would say. I'd heard some variation about a million times at bars, at which point I would pointedly say, *Yeah, my girlfriend thinks so, too,* even though I've been single for years.

"Anything weird with you?"

"*Weird with me*?" I ask, half-laughing.

"You know, your story. Ghosts. Does this kind of thing happen to you?"

"Things like this never happen to me. Or my family, as far as I know. Everyone's passed already, so I don't really have anyone to ask. But no word of mouth family lore."

Stevie's face grows surprisingly soft and sympathetic. It's a different look on her, but sweet. "I'm really sorry."

"Oh, it's okay. I came from a small family to begin with. Mostly just me and my mom. But as far as I know, no weird encounters in our family home in Topanga."

"California girl."

"Born and raised."

"You keep the house?"

I snort. "I did, actually. I haven't been able to figure out what to do with it. My house has an actual ghost, but that one has more figurative ones, I guess. I pay the taxes on it every year, but I haven't figured out what to do with it yet. I haven't really been back since my mom passed."

"Figurative might outweigh literal at this point," Stevie says gently. She's the first person other than my accountant to encourage me to go back to my roots in Topanga, mostly because I haven't told anyone about it—even Annalise. My mom passed years ago, two years into my time starring on my medical drama. It feels like a lifetime ago; my mom had gotten so sick so quickly, and so many things had changed so fast that I don't remember who I'd been before that. Even just talking about going back is overwhelming to me.

"So you agree that there's a ghost in my house?" I tease, desperately needing the topic of conversation to change.

"I think you believe there's a ghost in your house, which is more than enough."

I laugh, throwing my head back. "Way to totally not answer my question. That was really impressive."

She puts her hands up defensively, spinning from side to side in her chair. "I'm just saying."

"We'll see how tomorrow goes," I say, half-teasing Stevie's earlier sentiment. When Stevie and I lock eyes, my stomach flips and knots up. Even though I've made eye contact with what feels like a million people in my lifetime—friends, co-stars, family, reporters, my agent—this feels different. This is a new kind of eye contact that turns me completely upside down. I lose the ability to formulate a sentence instantly.

"So how was Wyatt County?" It's the only thing I can come up with, the only safe-feeling topic.

"Boring. Movies were always better. I was at the independent theater basically every weekend once I was old enough to drive."

"The t-shirt is pretty cool."

"Yeah, I didn't totally hate high school, so I kept some stuff from it," Stevie says.

"Just boring."

Stevie nods. "Exactly." She rolls her chair over the full five inches between us, filling the gap. I sit still and refuse to let her see how the smell of her cologne or shampoo or whatever it is she has on is completely driving me wild. I'm an actress; I'm supposed to be good at hiding things. But here I am, certain that everything I'm feeling and thinking is written all over my face.

Most likely because I'm secretly hoping Stevie will notice and make a move. But I can't admit that to myself yet.

"This is Humphreys Peak," Stevie says, pointing to part of the illustrated design on the shirt. She keeps her nails short and impressively well-maintained. Despite Stevie's generally messy appearance, it's obvious she's careful about her grooming. I've seen the hair products she has in her backpack; the look is intentional. And unfortunately effective in turning me on.

I look down at her hand, trying—and failing—to not get distracted by the thought of what her fingers would feel like inside of me.

"The outline of our main building," she continues, either completely unaware of how my breath has become stilted or relishing in it. She has to know that being this close to me and not actually touching me is a form is torture.

"Mhm," I say, the only thing I can contribute. My brain has gone radio silent otherwise, only able to think about how badly I want Stevie to kiss me.

She glances up at me through her surprisingly long eyelashes, and when our eyes meet, the air immediately changes. It's electric, thick in a way that makes it hard to breathe. We've never been this close together, this alone. I can see every single faint freckle dotted across her nose, the flecks of brown in her deep green eyes.

We're quiet and perfectly still. What feels like a lifetime passes with our eyes dancing over each other's faces and lips.

"You can kiss me." I barely raise my voice above a fragile whisper. I'm not a shy person, and I'm usually pretty good at reading cues on if someone is into me, so I'm not scared to say it. But I am scared the moment will shatter in an instant, like if I talk too loudly, reality will come crashing in, and we'll both realize this is probably a bad idea.

"Should I?" Stevie asks, her voice just as quiet.

"I want you to." My eyes flick down to her full lips. "I really want you to."

"But should I," Stevie says, a little more firmly this time. Less like a question and more like she's considering the different possible outcomes for her actions. Her eyes dance across my face, so full of longing. Even though we just met earlier today, she looks at me like she's been waiting for this moment for years. It was the same way I felt.

"Just once won't hurt. It doesn't have to be anything more than this. It doesn't have to change anything."

Her lips part, and warmth blooms between my legs. I'm practically crawling out of my skin for her.

"Just once," Stevie breathes, her eyes locked on my mouth.

Her leg brushes against my knee, and our eyes find each other again. At the same time, Stevie leans forward in her chair, and I lean forward from the bed. Our lips find each other, soft and curious.

Stevie kisses me so gently it's barely a whisper of anything. It feels like a true first kiss—high school style—and I like the lack of expectation. Even though we know where this is heading, she's not afraid to take her time with me. It makes me want her even more.

She stands up from her chair and leans over me, her hands on either side of my hips. I tilt my head up and kiss her, leaning back onto the bed. I open my mouth, telling her that I want more. I'm certain I've never wanted this more from anyone else before.

Now that we're here, like this, I can admit to myself just how into her I am. From the moment I first saw her, my brain and my body have slowly gone haywire. And now all that's left is pure want. I've always been so into confidence and certainty, and Stevie has it in spades.

I've struggled in the past with always picking the wrong ones because I'm so willing to chase ego and aloofness over stability. But the more I get to know Stevie, the more I realize that she's different from the people I've been with before. Different from what I assumed this morning when we met. She's not distant and cold and unfeeling; she's careful and focused and proud of her work. I don't know if my judgment is clouded by the minimal amounts of niceness she's directed at me—and the proximity and availability, if I'm being honest—but I hope I'll have more time with her to figure her out.

Stevie slides her knee between my thighs as she lies me completely flat on the bed. My heart is beating so fast I'm sure she can feel it.

She moves from my lips to the corner of my mouth to my jawline. Even as my nails dig into her back, she takes her time. Something about her not rushing this only turns me on more.

I get completely lost in the feeling of her against me, the smell of her skin, the softness of her shirt. I'm no stranger to something casual, but it feels different with Stevie. I feel so connected to her, so present in the moment. There's not one ounce of me that's going to wake up tomorrow and regret this.

She brings her hands up under my shirt, gently caressing over my stomach and hips. When her fingers find the hem, she pulls away. "Is this okay?" she asks, her voice low and sexy. I nearly blush at the hungry look in her eye.

"Yes," I answer, breathless, and she pulls my shirt—or I guess, her shirt—over my head. She drops it carefully onto the floor and takes a moment to look at me laid out on the bed. My nipples immediately harden in the cold hotel air.

"God, you are so beautiful," Stevie says, almost more to herself than to me. Her voice is just above a whisper, raspy with desire. I could listen to her say it on repeat for the rest of my life.

I pull her back down toward me, and she dips her face into my neck, her tongue gently gliding over my skin. Every nerve in my body feels like it's on fire. I'm so ready for her, so eager.

Stevie kisses down my chest and takes one of my nipples into her mouth, carefully using her tongue and her teeth. I cry out, arching my back in response.

"Stevie," I moan.

"I love the way you say my name," she says with a playful smile and moves to my left nipple, driving me wild all over again. Warmth floods between my legs, and I grind my hips against her, desperate for whatever I can get. Whatever she'll give me.

She reaches for the boxers I have on, and I lift my hips so it'll be easier for her to slip them off. She trails her hand down my stomach until she's just above my pubic bone.

"Can I?" she asks.

I nod—probably too enthusiastically—and Stevie positions herself on her knees on the floor. She pulls me to the edge of the bed, trailing kisses up the insides of my thighs until I'm panting. She puts the perfect amount of pressure on them, a buzz I've never experienced before exploding through me in response. This must be what it means when people talk about having *really* good sex. I've always been certain I've had it before, with an ex or a particularly giving one-night stand, but this is something else entirely. She's taking her time with me, making sure I feel every single sensation.

She moves from my right thigh to my slit, using her tongue to tease me open. When she flicks her tongue against my clit, I desperately grip the sheets, gasping her name. She puts her arms around my thighs and holds me in place, using her tongue and mouth with expert precision. She reads every reaction perfectly—knowing exactly where to put more pressure, where to stay for just a little bit longer. She quickly figures out what I like and what I don't. And then, when she figures out what I *really* like, she's careful to bring me close to the edge without letting me go over.

I'm completely lost to the sensation. Everything she does just makes me want her more.

It's hard to tell how much of the wetness between my legs is from me and how much of it is Stevie's spit. We've meshed into one—a mess of moaning and gripping and wanting more, more, more.

My back bows, my eyes rolling shut, when Stevie slips a finger inside of me as she flicks her tongue against my clit. I white-knuckle the comforter, spreading my legs further apart for more. She uses one finger and then two, bringing me right up to the edge before slowing down again.

She puts her free hand to my face, gently caressing my cheek and then trailing her thumb over my mouth.

"How are you feeling?" Stevie's voice is low and rough. If I were standing up, it would've been enough to make my knees weak.

I moan, unable to formulate words, and lean my face into her hand to take her fingers into my mouth. She's gentle at first, gauging my reaction. I open my mouth for her, trailing my tongue over her fingers, silently begging her to keep going. She complies, her eyes filled with the same lust that's roaring through me like wildfire.

She moves her other hand in and out of me quicker now, her tongue flicking just as fast against my clit. I'm wet in a way that defies science and my basic understanding of my own body. I'd never thought of ghost hunting as a form of foreplay, but now I'm starting to think there might be something to be said for it.

She slips her finger out of my mouth and carefully wraps her hand around my neck. She knows exactly where to hold her fingers, how much pressure to apply. Just enough to make me feel light and airy, but not so much that it cuts off my air supply.

"Oh my god, I'm gonna come," I cry out, unable to help myself. I hope the sound doesn't travel through the hotel walls the way I'm imagining it probably is. There's no way this is quiet, but a part of me doesn't care. If I'm only getting this once, I don't want her second-guessing for even a moment how good she's making me feel.

She thrusts deeper into me, my breasts bouncing from the motion. An orgasm rips through me, but I don't have any interest in asking Stevie to stop yet.

"Fuck, Lo," Stevie mumbles. I love watching her forearm flex as she continues fucking me. She takes her bottom lip between her teeth.

I keep my eyes locked on her. The hungry, desire-ridden expression on her face sends a wave of warmth through me all over again. Already, another orgasm starts to slowly build. "Keep going." My voice is breathy, unrecognizable. "Please, Stevie."

She does exactly as I ask, not changing her pace. I grip onto her hair, the sheets, whatever I can get my hands on in a futile attempt to stay grounded. I know with absolute certainty I've never been this turned on before. Sex in general has never felt like this with anyone before.

Despite the sexual nature of the TV show I was on, I've always considered myself someone who was fairly modest in bed. I don't normally like the vulnerability of someone seeing me naked and sprawled out. But it's different with Stevie; I feel hotter being so naked in front of her. She looks at me like I'm the most amazing thing she's ever seen.

Something almost inhuman takes over my body as I moan and writhe and cry out desperately, chasing the pleasure building inside me. She drops her head so her tongue is brushing against my clit, and I completely unravel.

"Stevie." My toes curl and my back lifts from the bed. "Oh my god. *Stevie.*"

My second orgasm is even more powerful than my first. It races through my entire body, my nerves tingling. It leaves me feeling weightless and breathless.

My skin feels so sensitive and exposed that my body tenses. Stevie slows down, easing her fingers out of me and lifting her head. She kisses up my body until she's hovering over me, a soft smile on her face. "How are you feeling?"

I chuckle. "Incredible." There's no use in lying—I don't even think I physically can after the sex we just had.

Stevie takes me into her arms. We fall back on top of the comforter, our bodies fitting together like two puzzle pieces. I rest my head on her chest, our arms wrapped around each other. I'm so completely at ease for what feels like the first time in forever.

"You're incredible," Stevie says, her voice just above a whisper. Her lips brush over my temple.

I look up at her, taking in the slope of her nose and her jaw and her surprisingly long eyelashes. She leans back onto the pillow, her eyes closed. I'm overwhelmed by how badly I want to kiss her, not even to initiate sex again, but just to be able to kiss her again. The way she touches me, holds me, treats me—I'm not ready for the night to be over yet.

And I can tell immediately that I'm completely and entirely fucked.

We can only have one time. That's it. That's what we agreed on. Do not *be the girl who agrees to just once and then gets her feelings hurt when she wants more.*

But as Stevie's hand brushes up and down my bare back, I know that can't possibly be it. Just because we promised one time doesn't mean only having sex one time—we can still take advantage of having the rest of the night.

I kiss Stevie's neck, pressing my body against hers all over again. She grips my thigh, turning her head so I can reach more of her neck.

"Yeah?" she teases.

"Mhm," I say, straddling her. I kiss up her neck to her ear. She moans, tightening her hands on my thighs.

"Come here." She turns us over so my back is flat on the mattress again, and I giggle, letting her take me away all over again.

10

STEVIE

We curl up together in bed, the sheets a tangled mess around us. I feel light and so happy I'm almost dizzy. I would never say it out loud to Lo, but I think—I *know*—that was the best sex I've ever had.

"Water?" I offer.

Lo nods. "Water would be perfect."

I reach over to the nightstand to pick up my reusable water bottle and hand it off to her. "I hope it's okay that it's mine. I can go fill up a cup for you, too, if you'd prefer that."

"I mean, we've already shared spit at this point," Lo teases. She sits up in bed, pulling the sheet up over her chest. I like seeing her like this—bare-faced, stripped down. Her perfectly maintained hair has transformed into the sexiest bed head I've ever seen.

She accepts the water and takes a sip as I slide back into bed with her. I pick up my phone to check the time—it's already almost three. I have no idea where the time went or how we got here, but I'm not complaining.

"You have a dog?" Lo asks and then blushes. "Sorry, I wasn't intentionally looking at your phone screen."

I smile. She's cute when she's nervous. "Yeah, he's four. I got him from the shelter when he was a few months old," I say, and make my phone light up again so she can see the picture better. "He joins us on out-of-state shoots. I usually just have a friend dog sit him if I'm still in town but busy with something work-related. Everybody loves him, so it's not hard to find someone to do it."

"He's cute," she says. "What's his name?"

Now it's my turn to blush. "Archie."

She throws her head back and laughs, and I can't resist smiling too. "That's cute."

"I have a tattoo of him, actually."

"That's even cuter," Lo gushes. "I have to see it."

"Here." I sit up and turn away from Lo so she can see the tattoo on my shoulder blade. "Can you see it?"

"Yeah, I love it." She puts her hand up to my skin, gently tracing her fingertips over it. It feels so foreign to be touched like this. I never let things go this far with anyone that the touch is comforting instead of inherently sexual.

I turn back to her and settle back in bed.

"What's this one?" she asks in a voice just above a whisper. Her fingers lightly trace over my forearm. It's usually covered by the sleeves of my oversized t-shirts, but it's plainly exposed right now.

I like the bubble we're in; it feels like we're the only two people in the entire world right now. Time isn't real and work isn't real. And for just a little longer, I can pretend Lo is just some girl that I know instead of a temporary co-star.

"Just a skull," I say, and then take her fingers, lightly dragging them over my skin. "Eyes, jaw, parietal. Nothing special," I added, predicting that would've most likely been her next question.

"I like it."

"None of my tattoos really mean anything—except for the one of Archie. I just like them."

She props her head up on her hand. "It's like something out of a sketchbook or something. It's cool."

"You have any tattoos?"

"I think you would've seen them by now if I did." Lo smirks, making me laugh.

I pull her in close, brushing my hand over her bare back. She slowly drops her head down onto my chest, like she's waiting for me to push her away. When I don't—I could never imagine—she relaxes her body completely against mine. Her arm hangs over my waist, our feet tangled up under the sheets.

"Just once," I mumble softly, mostly to remind myself that this can only happen once. It doesn't make sense for it to continue beyond this; I'm on the road too often, our schedules would never line up. There's a reason divorces and open relationships are so prominent in Hollywood.

Not that I'm imagining anything long-term would happen between me and Lo. Obviously.

"Just once," Lo says just as softly.

I can't tell if she really believes it or if she's lying, just like I am.

I wake up the next morning with Lo's naked body still wrapped up in mine. My alarm is blaring next to me, but Lo is entirely unaffected, her eyes still peacefully shut.

I'm tired in a way that makes my body feel like it's full of sand. My eyes are heavy, and I already know I have under-eye bags without needing to look.

I'll give myself exactly two more minutes to enjoy the warmth of Lo's body in the hotel sheets before I have to force myself out of bed. I'm careful not to move, not to even change the pace of my breathing, because I'm worried that'll somehow wake her up.

With my eyes glued to my phone to watch the time tick by, I realize I don't want it to end. I want these to be the longest minutes of my life in the best possible way.

But, eventually, the clock switches over to 8:42 a.m., and I know I can't give myself any longer than that. The second I start giving in and letting myself want to explore this further, the more I'm setting myself up for a long list of impossibly shitty outcomes.

I slowly peel myself away from Lo, one body part at a time, and then slip out of bed. She doesn't stir, which I don't mind. It seems easier for her to wake up when I'm already out of bed, so we don't have to navigate the complexities of realizing we'd slept so close when we have to spend all day together.

I move through my morning routine at a glacial pace, as if moving slower will somehow give me more time with Lo. But by the time I'm out of the shower and dressed, Lo is already awake and has made the bed.

"I'll go brush my teeth and we can get going," she says.

"Oh–" I say, caught off-guard. I catch myself immediately before a genuine protest can leave my lips. What the fuck am I on, wanting to spend more time with her? Wanting her to slow down? "Yeah. Based on the group chat, I think everyone's ready to get coffee."

"Awesome," Lo says. She steps up next to me, and I turn to give her space to walk by. For just a moment, the two of us hover there like we're not sure what to say to each other. But neither of us says anything. The spell is broken, and Lo continues to the bathroom, and I pack up my stuff.

After Lo brushes her teeth, we stand on either end of the room and look at each other. Lo looks down at her clothes. "I guess I can just wear this until we get back to my house? If that's okay with you? I can wash them, too."

"Oh, you don't have to worry about that," I say. "You can just give them back when we

"Thanks," Lo says. She freezes where she's standing, and we continue to look at each other like we're not sure what else there is to do or say. You would think we'd never met before last night.

And I guess we didn't really. This is the very definition of a one-night stand with someone I barely know.

It just feels different with Lo for some reason.

"Okay, let's go," I finally say and sling my backpack over one shoulder. There's no use in drawing out the discomfort; we might as well get the rest of the day moving.

"Ayo!" Andrew waves us over as we step outside. Andrew and the twins are near the van already, ready to go. "Let's get this bus moving."

It's obvious to all three of them at the same time that Lo is wearing my clothes. There might as well be a glowing sign above our heads that says *we had sex last night*. I ignore Andrew's eyes on me as I open the passenger side door for Lo and then head around to the driver's side.

"Alright, coffee and then back to Lo's," I say. "Then, Lo and I will go out to this, like, self-reflection meeting—"

"Self-connection," Lo corrects me.

"Self-*connection* meeting," I say. "Then, we'll film at her house and wrap at some point late tonight when we think we have enough stuff."

"You don't want any company visiting the cult? I can be the muscle," Andrew offers.

"I appreciate the offer, but I don't think we'll need muscle for this."

"We have to hang out in Lo's house all day?" Tanner asks as if that isn't his job.

"You guys have to get things set up for tonight. Cameras, lighting. We'll only be gone for a few hours, and then we need to be ready to film once it gets dark."

"Dude, the house is, like, freakishly haunted," Sean says.

"Then you'll get some good footage while you're setting up, too," I reply and start up the van.

I pull out of the hotel parking lot and drive us to the closest coffee shop I can map us to. The sun beats down on me through the windshield, almost making me forget that we've been deep in the throes of a paranormal investigation. So much of my job involves shadows and long overnight shoots that I forget to appreciate the sun when I have it.

I'm still not completely convinced of what's going on at Lo's house—everything feels like it can be disproven, like the kind of thing anyone could do with practical effects. I'm in the kind of business where most people watching the show are going to be trying to poke holes in every story we tell them. And as much as there are weird things happening at Lo's house, anyone who has been around the block with paranormal things knows how easy it is to make lights flicker and turn the house into a mess.

I pull the van into the coffee shop parking lot and park. "You already know what I want," I say to the twins, looking over my shoulder at them.

"Yes, boss," Tanner responds, saluting me in the process.

Even though I'm sending the twins in to get coffee—as has been tradition since Andrew and I have been able to take on interns, we also cover the cost of their coffees so it's more of a bit than a method of cruelty—I still get out of the car to stretch. Lo follows the twins, leaving just me and Andrew at the van.

As soon as Lo walks away, I can simultaneously breathe easier and also wish she were still standing next to me. I'm envisioning the day ahead and the drive up to the 'cult' house, and I'm a little nervous. I would just bring Andrew instead, but I don't want to leave Lo responsible for the twins.

And I also, selfishly, want just a little more time with her, even though I can tell that I'm being weird around her.

I can't tell if it's having sex with Lo or telling Lo things about myself that's making me feel so exposed around her now. I'm not typically someone who associates feelings with sex, especially something we both agreed would just be a one-off, so I'm guessing it's the latter. I'll fool around, but I never let anyone really get to know me.

Despite the show itself being fake, the story—and heart—behind it never was. I might not be a believer, but it feels almost like it's written into my family's bloodline to at least keep an open mind.

"So, how was your night?" Andrew asks, dragging out the syllables as he throws a glance my way. I realize I've been staring into the coffee shop, deep in thought about Lo, even though I can't even see her anymore.

"Good," I answer, hoping I can play it off effectively. I'm not in the business of kissing and telling, especially when it comes to Lo. I want our night to be our night and no one else's.

"Right." Andrew looks at me through his sunglasses. He scratches his beard. "She looks awfully cute in that Wyatt County t-shirt. Which, by the way, *you* went to Wyatt County High School, didn't you?"

"Shut up," I say, throwing a light punch into his arm.

Andrew knows me well enough to know that's everything he's getting out of me. "You ready for today? It's gonna be a big one."

"Yeah, I think so," I say. "Same thing we always do. Just another day at work."

"I don't know, man. I hate to say it because I don't really want it to be a ghost, but I think this might be something," Andrew says. "I know we should take advantage of Lo being away from the house, but I don't even think we need to set things up for this one. I think we'll be just fine."

I think it over, weighing our options. It makes me nervous to not set anything up and not guarantee that we'll get some good shots—otherwise, it'll be a waste of an episode—but I'm also worried Lo will see right through it. She's smart. Our practical effects are good on camera because we can make them good. But they won't hold up to someone in the room who isn't in on the act.

"Fuck it. Let's just film and see what we can get. We can edit stuff on the backend if we need to make it more interesting," I say. "If anything, this episode is more about Lo, anyway. People are watching for her."

Andrew is quiet for a beat. "Right," he finally says, his smile thick in his voice.

I turn to look at him. "What?"

"Nothing," Andrew says, shaking his head. "Nothing at all."

I brush off his comments, not ready to unpack that I am probably being way more obvious than I thought, and fix my eyes on the coffee shop door.

My phone vibrates, and I pull my phone out of my pocket. A notification tells me that Lauren Lane just paid me. Even though the account is nondescript and doesn't even have a profile picture—just like mine for privacy purposes—I don't have to check to know what it's for. I smile a little bit to myself, shaking my head.

Eventually, Lo comes back with the twins in tow. They're all carrying coffees, including the hot black coffee I asked for.

"Perfect, thank you," I say and pull it out of the drink carrier. The twins get into the car along with Andrew, and I turn to look at Lo. "How did you know exactly how much to send me for the room?" I ask.

"I looked up the rates online," Lo admits.

I laugh a little bit. "I guess this is on me for having a public Venmo profile."

"*Don't* try to send it back. I can already tell what you're plotting."

"I wasn't," I lie. I'll absolutely be sending the money back to her later today.

Lo throws me a smile over her shoulder before heading over to the passenger side of the van, leaving me weak in the knees.

11

LO

After grabbing coffee, we headed back to my house. There's an air of reluctance to get out of the car, evident amongst all of us. Even Stevie seems to be lingering in the van.

I look over at my house through the car window. It's so unassuming—sunny, bright, freshly painted. The yard is well-kept. It's not at all the scary, dilapidated house of horrors that makes appearances in movies and TV shows.

But even so, I can see the way only one of the curtains is moving—almost like there's someone in there, watching us.

"Alright, let's get moving," Stevie says.

I stare at the curtain, glued to it even as everyone else is climbing out of the van. Is she—or whatever ghost is living in my place—taunting us? Trying to get us out? I'll probably never know the answer unless the ghost decides to really lean into it and write something like *Get out!* on my wall.

"You coming?" Stevie asks, her voice muffled by her closed driver's side door.

I blink myself back to reality. You would think a ghost would become less scary the more time you spend around it, but I don't think I'm liking my ghost very much right now. "Yeah," I say.

With my hand poised over my buckle. I give myself three seconds to get up. Whether I like it or not, I own the house. My things are in there. I'll never downplay the amount of money I have, but I'm also not so wealthy that I can afford to leave all of my earthly belongings—and newly bought furniture—behind without hurting from it. Even if I sell the place, it'll be a long process, packing up again and moving.

"I'm going to change and then we can head out," I say as Stevie steps through the threshold. Andrew, the twins, and I are more hesitant, hovering just outside, until I finally take a deep breath and walk in.

After a night away, the slate has been wiped clean, and I'm on edge. I walk back into my house like there's an animal inside waiting to attack me. Months of going in and out with relative ease are suddenly completely forgotten, and I'm more afraid of this place than I've ever been. It definitely doesn't help that last night was the scariest night I've had in this house—or ever in my life.

I look down the hall, and Stevie looks at me. She waits for the boys to pass by before quietly asking, "Do you need an escort?"

Despite the time we had together last night—the life-changing, perfect, *I will* always *remember it in vivid detail* time—there isn't a hint of suggestion in her voice. She's not flirting with me; she's worried about me. And it makes sense since I'm not exactly doing a good job of hiding my fear.

"I…" I weigh my options, thinking of the probably hundreds of times I've gone into my bedroom and changed, the times I'd been alone. I'm capable of doing it. I know I am.

But the way my heart is racing tells me that I don't think I can go back to that. Despite Stevie's certainty that there's an explanation for everything, I don't think it's as simple as a mechanical issue.

"Yeah." Her eyes, the same green eyes that gazed at me so lovingly last night, meet mine. "Can you come with me?"

She nods, and I'm thankful she doesn't say anything about it. We head toward the bedroom. The boys are either too distracted with setting up cameras or too smart to ask questions; they don't make a comment as we slip down the hall just the two of us.

"It's nice to be in here when Fleetwood Mac isn't playing at the highest possible volume it can be played at."

I snort as I head over to my dresser and then the closet. I've never been so grateful that I've been keeping up with my laundry.

Not that I care at all what Stevie thinks of me. Or my outfits.

I drop my clothes on the bed and pull my shirt over my head. I'm calmed by the warm rays of light coming through the windows and the gentle silence of the house. Moments like this remind me of exactly why I wanted to live here so badly in the first place, and why all of the additional mess—like fearing for my life—is worth it. For just a second, I can pretend that I'm not constantly on high alert being here.

I pull Stevie's shirt over my head and gingerly place it down next to my pile of fresh clothes.

"I, um." Stevie turns away, her face pink.

"It's nothing you haven't seen before, it's okay." I smile a little bit, changing quickly so Stevie can take herself out of the corner of my room she's stuffed herself into.

Despite the strange comfort and closeness wearing Stevie's clothes brought to me, I'm grateful to be back in my own things. Clothes have always been one of my biggest vices outside of books. I immediately feel more like myself with my favorite pair of jeans on.

"Okay," I say, smoothing down my hair and slipping earrings into my ears. I don't bother with anything more than mascara and a touch of lip gloss, mostly because I'm ready to leave the house again. I've been weighing my options on Stevie's offer to not film with them tonight and instead leave it to the experts, but I feel too deep into all of this to pull back now.

Stevie turns around to look at me, half turning her head and then fully committing when she sees I've pulled on a loose-fitting pair of jeans and a partially buttoned black cardigan. I'd be lying if I said I didn't pick this outfit because I thought she might like it.

Her eyes travel over the outfit and over my face. "You look great," she says softly, and it's a more meaningful compliment than I've ever gotten before. All of the times I've heard that I was beautiful, talented, sexy, whatever, pale in comparison to her earnest tone.

I fight off a blush. "Thanks." I think about her voice in my ear last night and the way her arms felt around me. Even though the sleeve of her t-shirt is covering her upper arms now, I can still picture exactly where her tattoos are.

I check to make sure I have the necessities—phone, wallet, lip gloss—and then head for my bedroom door. Stevie follows behind, closing my bedroom door most of the way behind us.

"Ready to brave the trek out of town?" I ask.

"No, but I'll do it for the story," Stevie responds. "I'm intentionally picking a place not in a major city after this."

I snort. "Can't get out of here fast enough."

"It's nice to get a break sometimes, even though I do like it out here. I like being on the road."

"I get that. I've done a few movies on location, and it's not a vacation by any means, but—"

I stop when, out of the corner of my eye, I see the door to my bedroom move. It's subtle, opening slowly like someone is pulling it open from behind the door where we can't see.

My blood turns to ice. Stevie puts a protective arm out around my waist like she's ready to push me out of the way at any second if she needs to.

The door doesn't creak or moan—the house is too newly updated for the typical creepy old sounds—but the silence is almost scarier. I can hear the faint voices of the boys and the clamor of them setting things up down the hall. But there's nothing else. No footsteps, no indication that a living person is in my room.

Even so, Stevie takes a tentative step forward, peeking into my bedroom from a distance to investigate. The door is fully open now, as if we hadn't just closed it. I know with certainty that none of the windows are open, and there's no random draft to explain why the door would move.

I cross my arms tightly around my body, fighting off the urge to sprint and leave Stevie to face whatever might be waiting for her.

Her hand sits on the door handle for a long beat before she finally yanks the door away from the wall, looking behind it as if someone is going to be standing there. I can assume, based on her reaction, that no one is.

"Stevie?" I try not to sound as freaked out as I am, but I'm definitely failing. The warm sunlight pouring out from the bedroom into the hallway is incongruous with my racing heart and sweaty palms.

She scans my bedroom, moving her head slowly from left to right before walking back down the hallway toward me. "There's no one there."

"Of course there isn't," I say, trying to play off my fear as annoyance. I'm not doing a good job.

We say goodbye to the boys and then head out for the day, leaving us with just enough time to make it to the building where the Self-Connection meetings are held. Our goal is to get there early so we can grab Sunniva before she gets distracted by whatever her meetings entail.

As we're driving—Stevie in the driver's seat—my phone rings in my lap.

"It's Annalise." Stevie gives a little nod of acknowledgement, telling me she doesn't mind if I answer.

"How's the ghost hunt? Get any proof yet?"

"Things are fine," I say, holding my phone to my ear. "Some weird shit has been going down, though. I don't even know where to begin with telling you about all of it. It doesn't seem like the ghost is thrilled with having people in the house filming."

"Do you think you're just, like, the ghost's favorite or something? It seems like they only like you and then chase everyone else out. Except me. But I only ever stop by for, like, an hour at a time because your house gives me the creeps."

"I know you're fucking with me, but that might not be an unreasonable guess. We don't really know anything at this point. The most I can say is that things are getting really weird."

"Good thing you have experts around to help."

"For sure," I agree.

"Speaking of, how are things going with Stevie?" Annalise asks, a teasing tone to her voice. I immediately turn closer to my door and cup my hand over my phone, just in case the sound is traveling enough for Stevie to hear. I haven't had the chance to catch up with her yet, so she doesn't know the full story, but

Stevie wouldn't know that. For all she knows, I've been texting Annalise for hours, giving her play-by-play on how the sex was.

I drop my voice lower as if Stevie won't be able to hear me from her seat next to me. "In the car with me."

"Just you two?"

I urgently need to redirect this conversation. "Things are going really well. We're meeting up with a former owner of the house to see if she might know anything."

"So things are going well with the hot paranormal investigator?"

From next to me, Stevie does a terrible job at hiding her amused grin.

"Things are fine here. We're doing the big investigation tonight, and then the team is off to the next shoot." Even though it's obvious Stevie can hear Annalise clear as day through my phone speaker, I'm not letting myself get embarrassed that easily. I'll avoid Annalise's questions in whatever way I have to.

"Well, text me with updates. And just know I'll be disappointed if you don't at least get her number."

Annalise hangs up, and I put my phone face down in my lap.

Stevie isn't even trying to hide the shit-eating grin on her face. "She's nice."

"Shut up," I grumble, smiling, and Stevie laughs.

The building that Sunniva hosts her Self-Connection meetings out of doesn't look like much more than a family home tucked into a suburban neighborhood. Every house is built similarly, and all of them are done up in tans and yellows and browns. Lawns are perfectly manicured and are a perfect lush green. In the distance, I can see the tops of mountains. There's not much else in the immediate area; sidewalks lead in and out of the neighborhood, but they don't seem to go anywhere.

"Do you think this Self-Connection stuff is super lucrative, or do you think there's family money behind this?" I can't judge—my mom and her parents were connected to filmmaking for the entirety of their careers and were paid well for it. My former TV job paid for a lot of my house, but the inheritance I'd had sitting in my savings for years definitely helped.

"Who knows—all I know is any amount of money going toward this woman is probably too much."

"This is not what I was expecting," I admit.

"What, you imagined some, like, massive compound in the middle of nowhere? We're still basically in Los Angeles," Stevie teases.

"I know, it just looks so...plain. It's like trying to explain to someone that my house is haunted. It doesn't have that look."

"Probably because it's not actually a cult like you're suspecting," Stevie says. "I'm sure she's just some self-aggrandizing woman who was told one too many times that she's *really* good at reading people."

"She read one too many books about psychology and assumed that she could be a therapist without the formal training," I say, playing along even though I'm not feeling as certain as Stevie. Something in my gut is telling me that this is some form of a cult—or at the very least, a group that is into some *very* odd shit.

I've seen more than a few people in my acting circle get sucked into all kinds of things, most of them framed as a way of finding themselves or staying true to themselves despite the materialism around them. One or two went from curious to deeply wrapped up, most of their conversations coming back to spirituality in an empty, selfish way—typically with the goal of improving their careers and not actually wanting to be a better, more self-aware person.

I've never had strong feelings one way or another about spirituality or religion. I've gotten my tarot cards read a few times and prayed other times, usually out of desperation for my mom to get better. But I've seen the ways it can be used to reel people in, the harm that it can cause when influence and power are misused, and that's the part that I do have strong feelings about.

There are a decent number of cars on the street, but it's hard to tell if they're neighbors or here to see Sunniva. Stevie parks behind one in an empty spot a few houses down from the address we're supposed to be going to.

"We're not going to get murdered here, right?" I ask.

She shrugs, looking around. "I mean, I don't think so."

"I don't know if that's super comforting, actually."

Stevie pushes open her car door. "It'll be fine—come on."

The sun is already starting to fade in the sky, suggesting late afternoon is around the corner. Just like most days in Southern California, there's barely a cloud in sight.

We walk down three houses and then head up the empty driveway to the house listed online.

"Are we supposed to just walk in?" I whisper as we head up toward the front door.

"I'd assume so," Stevie says. As we step up onto the front stoop, the front door opens. I jump nearly a foot in the air, gripping Stevie's arm in fear.

"Hello," a woman—who isn't Sunniva based on the website, unless Sunniva is now suddenly in her sixties—greets us. "New faces. We're so happy to have you. Welcome."

"Thank you," I say, an impulsive response to kindness, even though I'm not sure I'm particularly grateful to be here. Something about this neighborhood, this house, this group, is making me really uneasy.

She steps aside so we can come in. The house isn't packed, but it's decently busy. It looks like a standard family home—wood floors, art on the walls. The decorations are tasteful, if not a little like something straight out of a catalogue.

"How did you hear about us?" she asks. I press my lips together. Stevie and I stupidly didn't come up with a backstory of any kind; I'm now seeing what a bad idea that was.

"Online. We've been facing some internal demons, and we're hoping this might help," I say before Stevie can answer. I trust her to take care of business, but I also *really* don't want eyes on us. Coming across as an outsider in a setting like this feels really risky.

Or maybe I've just listened to one too many crime podcast episodes.

"Where can we find Sunniva?" Stevie asks.

"Oh, I'm sure she's wandering around. Can I get you anything? Water, a snack? We're about to get started."

"We're fine, thank you." Unsurprisingly, Stevie is skilled at being direct but gentle. The woman doesn't look offended—or like she suspects anything weird from us. She earnestly just believes we're here to join one of the meetings or become a member of her group or whatever.

She heads off to go chat with someone else in the house, and we move through the open floor plan. Stevie's eyes travel across the room, moving over faces.

"There," I say, spotting a woman walking up the stairs with the same bone structure and hair as Sunniva from the video. "I think that's her."

Stevie and I cut across the living room and follow her. "Sunniva?" Stevie asks. I resist the urge to shush her, the reality of what we're doing just now sinking in. We drove all this way to talk to this woman at her house. We have no idea what she's capable of, no idea what these meetings entail. We could've easily just walked into the lion's den without even realizing.

Sunniva turns to greet us when she reaches the top of the stairs. Stevie and I stand about halfway up, close enough to her to smell her perfume. "Hello. New faces—wonderful to see," she says with a smile. "Typically, I don't have guests come up here during these meetings, but I assume you're doing this for a reason."

"Yeah, we have a few questions for you," Stevie says.

Sunniva looks amused more than anything. She crosses her arms, tilts her head. "Okay," she says. She looks simultaneously older and younger in person—she's gotten light touch-up work done to her face, and has streaks of silver through her hair that I couldn't see in her video online. Her clothes are loose and clearly expensive, a silk wrap-around that goes to her ankles that she wears over a dress. It's impossible to guess how old she is—maybe a younger-looking fifty, maybe an older-looking thirty.

"I bought your old house," I say. "We never met during the process, but I found your name in the paperwork I have."

"Off of West Belford?"

"Yes," I confirm. Having Sunniva's attention makes me nervous, like everything I'm saying is somehow the wrong answer.

"Beautiful house. I hope you're enjoying it—we were sad to leave, but it wasn't large enough for us anymore."

"It is really beautiful, but there have been some..." I look for the words, but my brain goes numb as Sunniva's deep brown eyes bore into me. "Odd things happening. Unexplainable things. And I was wondering if you had similar experiences."

Sunniva is quiet for a moment. "Why did you come find me?"

There's no use in hedging around the truth. "There's something really horrible in that house."

She's quiet again and then waves us down the hallway, deeper into her house. It's not very large—the upstairs is more compact than the downstairs. There are doors lining the walls, some of them open and some of them not. It's impossible to determine how many people live here, if anyone does at all. It could just be where Sunniva holds her meetings. And based on how it doesn't seem like there are any personal items anywhere in the house—no photos, no mess, no collectibles—I'm guessing that might be the case. I wonder if she'd used my house the same way.

She goes into what must be the primary bedroom based on the size and opens the closet door. "Did you look into what we do here before you came?"

"A little bit," I admit. "But not extensively."

"I work in spiritual healing. That's why we're all here—my friends downstairs are all working through their own personal struggles. They'll come in group settings or sometimes one-on-ones. It's important work; I argue that it's necessary work."

She pulls out a folder of papers from the closet—not what I was expecting, but then again, I don't think anything Sunniva does is predictable—and shuts the door.

"Part of the healing and self-discovery process is working through those complicated feelings that often consume us—grief, jealousy, anger. We use various methods to let those go so we can keep living our lives and, ideally, find some form of peace. I'm sure any of my friends here would be happy to give a glowing recommendation. We've seen tremendous progress from people who've finally been able to get closure."

"Closure," Stevie says slowly. "How does that work? Journaling?"

Sunniva heads for the door to leave the room, and we follow behind her, our feet padding over the pristine carpet. "Oh no, we specialize here in gaining closure for those who've been hurt by someone they can't make contact with," she says as she keeps up her pace a few paces ahead of us. "Typically, this is someone who has already passed."

I know I'm going to regret asking the question, but someone has to ask it. "How can you get closure from someone who's dead?"

Sunniva turns and looks at me, stopping me and Stevie in our tracks. She stops so quickly that we nearly run into her. I don't like the look in her eye; it's as if she can literally see through me, see what I'm thinking and feeling. "We have our methods. We can try some, if you'd like."

Then, she starts walking again, leaving me and Stevie to exchange looks of *What the fuck is this woman on?*

"She must not have seen Hereditary," Stevie whispers, making me snort. I quickly cover up the sound with a cough.

"We'll pass on that, but thank you," Stevie says in response to Sunniva's offer. I'm glad she's the one answering the question instead of me; she's firmer than I'm capable of being, and I have a feeling it requires a strong personality to keep up with Sunniva. She's been soft-spoken and gentle so far, but it's becoming increasingly obvious she has ways of being convincing when she wants to be.

"Are you sure?" She turns her head over her shoulder to look at me. "You've lost your mother. You wouldn't want one last opportunity to speak with her?"

My mouth goes dry, my stomach immediately drops. I'm not naive enough to give her information—I know that she'll just keep making educated guesses to make me think that she can read my mind or something—but it's hard to keep a level reaction when that's the last thing I expected her to say. I don't talk about my mother's passing: I've never posted about it online, and I don't talk about it in interviews. I've kept it between me and my grief counselor and my therapist and my desperate Google searches following hours of crying so hard I almost vomit.

"She's fine," Stevie answers, and I reach out to squeeze her hand in a silent thanks.

"She misses you," Sunniva continues, definitely taking advantage of the fact that I'm the weaker link. I can suddenly hear my mother's voice, her laugh. I'm so fortunate to have so many photos and video recordings of her; I'll never forget any of it. Bringing her back up like this makes me crave her company—just one more coffee together on her porch, another morning of sitting on her bed while she spritzes on her perfume as a finishing touch.

I try to channel Stevie's skeptical energy and the way she still questions everything, even when it feels so clearly laid out. She's always looking for more proof, more evidence. I'm not about to believe that this woman actually has some kind of ability to not only know about my mother, but also speak to her.

But it is a really strange coincidence she would know, and that's what makes me uneasy.

"We really should stay on topic. We don't want to take too much of your time," Stevie says.

"The best way to understand our practices here is via demonstration." Sunniva keeps her attention on me, clearly waiting for me to be the one who breaks.

"A verbal explanation works just as well in this case." Stevie comes to my rescue again.

"I can explain it to you, but you won't believe it until you see it," she says. She stops at the top of the stairs. "If you're planning on staying for the meeting—which I encourage—you'll see some of the lighter practices we work on. Most of those have to do with the self, as implied by the name. But we do other sessions, too, that are more personalized. Even when you think there's nothing to be said to someone, there always is. We open those doors for people."

"What do you mean by lighter practices?" Stevie asks.

"We encourage self-reflection, talking, and drawing. We discuss personal areas of improvement. Hurt that we've experienced at the hands of others."

"So, group therapy?"

Sunniva offers an amused smile. "Something more than that."

"And the individual sessions? How are those conducted?" I ask.

"It depends on what someone is looking for. For you, I would tell you to bring something of your mother's that meant something to her. And then we would try and reach her."

"Are you a medium, then?" Stevie asks. She says the word *medium* like someone just asked her about the Easter Bunny.

She lifts a shoulder in a shrug. "There are a lot of words people could use."

"And you did these practices at the place you just sold?"

"Of course."

"Did you see anything or talk to anyone during that time? Maybe invite someone into the house?"

"Well, a lot of what we do involves inviting someone into the house, love. That's how we speak to them. They can't just walk back into our realm; someone has to bring them here."

Next to me, I can practically feel Stevie's desire to roll her eyes radiating off of her. I'm less certain, though. As much as something about Sunniva doesn't sit well with me, it would explain a lot. It's not that there's a ghost that's just been in my house all this time; she intentionally brought someone inside.

"Who did you invite into the house?"

"We communicate with sometimes five or six different people over the course of a day. It could be anyone. Maybe there are multiple spirits still living in your home."

Perfect. "And this has been helpful for people?"

"Absolutely. Some people will come for regular sessions to talk to someone. We can't always reach them, but we usually can. It's a specialty of mine."

"But how do you get them to leave?" I ask. "How can *I* get them to leave?"

"Sometimes, you can't," Sunniva says. "That's not my line of business. People tend to want them to stay where they can find them again."

I don't say what feels obvious to me—that people making repeat visits to speak to a loved one who passed doesn't sound particularly healthy. And Sunniva being the middleman to it all definitely makes it feel weird and more exploitative than helpful.

"None of this is scary. I can show you how it works. We can use your mother's purse," Sunniva says.

My stomach drops. "This isn't hers," I lie, an instinct to keep her as far away from my mother as possible. As much as I love and miss her, and would do anything to have her back, I don't want to play this game. The more Sunniva says, the less I like what she's doing and the less I like her.

Sunniva doesn't seem discouraged. Rather than behaving how I'd imagine a bullshitter would, she gives me a look of certainty. It's like she really does somehow know it's my mom's purse, which isn't possible. It could be a lucky guess again, but my purse isn't vintage—it's less than a decade old; my mom bought it just before she died, so it's not a safe bet.

My stomach turns. Having a ghost in my house is one thing—especially since it seems like it was invited in rather than just deciding to haunt the place willingly—but whatever Sunniva is engaging in doesn't sit right with me. It doesn't feel safe for someone like her to know anything at all about me.

"Can we see how you talk to them?" Stevie looks at me like I've suddenly grown a second head.

Sunniva doesn't hesitate. She waves us down the stairs and we follow behind. Stevie stops me at the top of the stairs, her hand around my upper arm.

"What are you doing?" she asks through gritted teeth.

"I have to see what's going on here." I can't bring myself to say the whole truth—that I'm starting to believe Sunniva does actually have some kind of paranormal ability, and I need to be proven wrong. I need to see the bells and whistles, the way she fakes people out. I want to know that her empire is built on a lie, rather than going home believing that a woman really does hold so much power.

"Nico," Sunniva calls out when she makes it to the bottom of the stairs. She does a dainty wave to get his attention and bring him over to her.

Nico is an almost shockingly handsome man with a full head of silver hair and glowing skin. He's tall and fit and looks annoyingly good with Sunniva—they'd be the perfect, beautiful couple if Sunniva didn't put such a bad taste in my mouth.

"How can I help you?" he asks.

"Our two new friends would like a demonstration of one of our calls. Can you get my things set up for me, please? We'll change up the plan for today's meeting, just for a little bit." She rests a hand on his upper arm, and he glows.

"Of course."

Nico walks off, and Sunniva guides us into the living room, where people have started gathering around the room. Rather than a circle like I'd seen in my grief groups, all of the seating faces the front of the room.

"We have some new faces here, as well as some faces who I know have only come to these meetings instead of doing solo sessions with me. As a way of introducing you to the other things that we offer here, I'd like to do a demonstration." Despite the smile on Sunniva's face, I can't help but think about how there is something so sinister about her mannerisms and attitude.

I seem to be the only other person in the room who feels that way—other than Stevie, who's watching this all play out from next to me with an amused smirk. Everyone else is staring at her with wide, attentive eyes, listening eagerly like every word Sunniva says is the most important thing ever uttered.

"We're all on board with this?" she asks. Everyone sitting in the living room nods, and Nico approaches her with

"Paulina, would you like to speak to your son?"

Chills climb up my back. A woman looks at Sunniva like she can't tell if this is a cruel joke or not. She stands up, her hands visibly shaking as she puts them to her mouth in disbelief.

"Right now?" she asks. She looks like she's in her forties, her brown hair pulled back into a shiny ponytail. She wears loose-fitting jeans and a shirt that's practically falling off her thin frame. It's not until she reaches the front of the room and stands next to Sunniva that I can see the details of her face—the bags under her eyes, her sunken cheeks. I recognize the grief that's written all over her because I've been there. Some days, I'm still there.

Sunniva nods. She takes Paulina's hand and gives it a squeeze. "He's been asking for you."

"And I can still see him next week, like we scheduled?"

"Of course. But if I can bring you two together again sooner, it's my duty to offer that," Sunniva says. There's fake warmth in her voice.

"What the hell is going on?" Stevie whispers, leaning closer to me so I can hear her.

I shrug, unable to offer anything at all. I might believe there's a ghost in my house, but I'm a lot more skeptical that this woman somehow has the ability to speak to all of these people. It's almost definitely an elaborate scheme, the equivalent of a teenager pulling out an Ouija board and pretending the pieces are moving on their own. Except this woman is charging what has to be an absurd amount of money per 'session.'

Nico shuts the curtains, and the house goes almost completely dark in an instant, other than some lamps that have been left on. Everyone is quiet as Sunniva delicately sets her things up at a small table—papers from the folder she grabbed upstairs, a candle, a small stone. She sits down, and Paulina sits down across from her. From here, we can see everything—neither

Sunniva nor Paulina are shielding anything. We have a perfect view into what they're doing, which will make it easier to figure out how Sunniva has been fucking with everyone.

"First, we're going to invite Bobby in," Sunniva explains, looking out to the crowd of eight or so in the living room. They're a captive audience—not one fidget, not one sound. She turns her attention to Paulina. "Do you have something of Bobby's?"

"Always," Paulina says in a soft, mousy voice. She grabs her purse, fumbling through the motions of grabbing something from inside. She pulls out a well-loved baseball, still green with grass. "Something told me to bring this in particular today. I'm glad I did."

Sunniva smiles knowingly. I resist the urge to vomit.

Sunniva picks up a box of matches from the table and strikes one. She holds it over the candle until it lights and then shakes out the match, leaving the candle to burn. The candle has been clearly used before, dried wax stuck down the sides in frozen streams.

She closes her eyes, and Paulina does the same. Her mouth moves, but she doesn't seem to be saying anything; it's so quiet in the house we'd be able to hear her if she were.

She opens her eyes and turns back to her audience. Her eyes travel over toward me and Stevie in the process. The look in her eye is one of certainty and confidence, as if she knows I've been doubting her and she can't wait to prove me wrong. "Once we welcome Bobby, we're going to ask him some questions. He'll use this stone right here to answer our questions. We keep them strictly to yes or no, but sometimes, someone will speak to us."

Stevie and I glance at each other.

Bullshit, she mouths.

"Bobby, are you with us? Can you hear me?" Sunniva asks in her sickeningly sweet, fake therapist voice. "Can you blow the candle out for me, Bobby? Just like you've done before. Let us know you're here."

Of course, it would be a candle to signal the presence of a ghost—it's the easiest thing to fake. A gentle breeze would be enough to convince someone that there's some kind of paranormal presence in the room.

"Bobby? Baby? It's mommy," Paulina says. I can hear how tight her throat is and how hard she's fighting off tears. My stomach knots.

Everyone—me and Stevie included—holds our breath, waiting to see if anything is going to happen. My eyes are carefully studying the scenery of the room for any kind of setup. Maybe a light, intentional breeze, maybe Nico will do something, maybe Sunniva has a way of getting the candle to blow out.

The fire at the tip of the candle suddenly begins to move, jumping left to right and then firmly to the left.

I reach out for Stevie's hand. Even though I believe Sunniva is a bullshitter through and through, I've never seen fire behave like that unless there's a breeze—and there's no breeze in the house. Not even a draft is coming through the closed doors or windows.

Maybe sitting in on this was a really, really bad idea after all.

Paulina nods frantically. "Good job, Bobby. I'm here. Whenever you're ready. I want to listen."

A chill passes through me, and my shoulders shake as I violently shiver.

Then, the flame goes out.

I grip Stevie's hand even harder, startled. I look around for an explanation, but I can't see anything. Nico hasn't moved, and there's no air coming from any of the vents. There are no fans, no open windows.

"Bobby," Paulina cries, relief evident in her voice. "Bobby. Hi, baby. I heard you've been missing me; I've been thinking about you, too. I saw your uncle for the first time since you died. He's so, *so* sorry."

Paulina is so caught up that she doesn't even seem to realize that we're all still here and listening to her. She's only talking to Bobby.

"Do you have any questions for Bobby?" Sunniva asks.

"Um." Paulina wipes away tears pooling in her eyes. "Bobby—do you remember Uncle James? They're moving now, your aunt and uncle. They couldn't handle living at the house anymore, not with the pool. It was too much."

The pieces are starting to come together for me: Sunniva is silent the entire time and letting Paulina fill the space. Paulina is certain she's speaking to her dead son, but it's probably just Sunniva setting her up to believe that. It's so simple but genius, in a terrible, evil kind of way. Sunniva doesn't have to do anything but make the people around her believe that it's real.

"You can just move the stone to tell us, Bobby. We're here," Sunniva says. "Do you remember your aunt and uncle?"

The house is quiet, and some people even lean forward in their seats to get a better look at the table.

The stone moves the tiniest bit on the table, and I nearly jump a foot into the air. When it starts moving across the table, far to the right, I duck the tiniest bit behind Stevie. It's like watching a horror movie play out in real time. The deeper Sunniva and Paulina get into it, the more I want to cover my eyes and pretend it's not happening.

"Good job, Bobby," Sunniva says. "Thank you for letting us know you remember them."

Paulina nods, her face still crumpled with tears. "Do you...do you forgive them? Do you forgive me?"

"He's told us before he forgives you," Sunniva says gently, placing a hand on Paulina's forearm.

I study the table, desperate for any kind of explanation. But the bottom of the table is exposed, so I'd know if Sunniva was somehow moving it from below. And no one's hands have gone anywhere near it. And then, most obvious of all, a stone isn't light enough to move with just a soft breeze. There has to be physical force of some kind.

Paulina sobs into her hands. "I'm so sorry, baby. I'm so sorry. I should've been watching you better. You were so young. You couldn't swim."

The woman bawls, her bottom lip trembling so hard it looks like it's vibrating. My eyes burn with tears, and I shake my head. I hate this. I hate watching what she's doing to that poor woman. And I hate—*hate*—that I'm watching obvious exploitation of grief in real time. It's all too much.

I can't help it—I storm out of the house before I can even think twice. I yank the front door open, flooding the entryway with light, and blink away the sun. As I walk, I blink my eyes in an attempt to readjust to the light outside.

I have too many thoughts and feelings swirling around inside of me to make sense of any of it. I can't tell what's real and what isn't.

But mostly, I hate that it all *felt* real. Even though I logically refuse to believe Sunniva was actually communicating with a ghost child named Bobby, I can't come up with an explanation to the contrary.

Stevie follows quickly behind me, unlocking the car from a distance. I throw myself dramatically into the passenger seat, crossing my arms. Stevie walks up calmly to the driver's side door and opens it.

"Do you want to talk—"

"She's evil! She's literally evil!" I throw my hands up in the air.

"I agree, it's fucked up."

I'm seething—an emotion I rarely, if ever, experience. Even when it comes to acting or the loss of my mom, I never hold onto a grudge. I don't let myself dwell on what ifs, don't let myself get angry over losing out on a role, or how unfair it is that my mom got sick. It's part of life. Holding too tightly onto it all makes me feel like a balloon ready to burst, and I can't do that to myself.

But the only thing Sunniva's whole charade is making me feel is pure, unfiltered anger.

"She's taking advantage of them!"

"She is."

"And bringing up my mom!" I try to think of anything else to say, but I can't. There aren't enough words in the English language—in any language—to express how frustrated I am.

"I don't know how she knew that about my mother," I say, my voice softer now. My emotional outburst leaves my body just as quickly as it entered. I fight off tears. "I've been wracking my brain to make sense of it, and I just can't. I don't know how she would've known. She didn't even know we were coming today, so it's not like she could've done a deep dive on me and found, like, an obituary or anything."

Stevie takes my hand and I realize I've been ripping into the skin around my fingernails. I haven't done that since my mom was still alive.

"It was unfair of her to bring it up either way." Stevie's voice is gentle. I'm surprised she's not immediately shooting it down and telling me I'm being an idiot for falling for anything Sunniva said or did. Or that I'm an idiot for bothering to get upset about any of it.

Between her soft words and touch, I have to remind myself that isn't a thing between me and Stevie. We might've had sex last night—into this morning—and her touch might be really nice and her words are so comforting, but I'm *not* going to go there. I'm not going to be the girl who thinks too much into it and gets hurt.

"Something about all of this feels really terrible, though, right? Like, weird?" I gnaw on my bottom lip. "Whether all of this is actually real or not...I don't know. I don't have the ability to know. But the way she's using it, this approach of having basically unlimited access to ghosts or pretending to and exploiting loved ones and the deaths of loved ones..."

"It's gross, I agree. And I think it might catch up to her eventually. I've seen enough horror movies to know people usually can't get away with playing with stuff like this for too long."

I smile a little bit. Stevie smiles, too, tilting her head down so she can look me in the eyes.

I move my hand away from Stevie's, suddenly nervous from how intimate this moment feels. Stevie's face remains unreadable and neutral—probably because I *am* actually thinking too much into this moment and the handholding was purely platonic. "Was this enough to finally convince you my house is haunted?"

"It's a compelling argument—all of it does feel like a strangely perfect explanation. But I don't know if I'm sold on Sunniva having some means of communicating with the other side. Or whatever." Stevie thinks it over for a beat, quiet from next to me. "Actually, I think I know exactly who can be our translator for whatever the fuck just went on in there."

Stevie lifts her hips so she can pull out her phone from her back pocket. She clicks around and then puts the phone on speaker.

"Hello," a voice that is distinctively Valerie's rings out. She drags out each syllable of the word, making me smile.

"Hey—it's Stevie. Question for you."

"Bring it on."

"We just met with that woman from the website and she's...pretty intense," she says, keeping her eyes fixed straight ahead through the windshield instead of looking my way. "I guess she's some kind of medium and she can, like, speak to the dead."

"Hm," Valerie says. "And we have reason to believe this is true?"

"Does it help that we saw her do it?" I ask. "Or, like, supposedly saw her do it?"

"I mean, yeah." She's quiet for a beat. "How did she speak to them?"

"Some kind of spiritual practice, I guess. It seemed almost witchy. She had this, like, homemade Ouija board kind of thing." Stevie still talks with her hands even over the phone. Even through all my frustration with Sunniva, I find it deeply charming.

"I mean, some people theorize that you only find evil spirits in Ouija boards. They wait until someone is stupid enough to invite them in and then enter our realm from there."

"So you think the ghost living in my house is evil?"

"There's really no way to know. Have you asked the ghost?"

"We haven't exactly gotten around to it," Stevie deadpans.

Valerie is unaffected. "There's a decent chance she brought something into your house that can't leave. Or maybe just won't leave, which is the scarier option because it raises the question of why. Did you get any insight into who it could be?"

"Just that it could be basically anyone. She said she talks to five or six spirits a day. It sounds like people have been using her as a resource for this shit for years, and Lo's house used to be the hotspot."

"It could be anyone," Valerie says.

"Yeah, that's what I just said," Stevie responds.

"No, I mean—it could be *anyone*. Just because those are the people she tried to speak to doesn't mean those are the only people she spoke to. Or who she actually spoke to. Like I was saying, some spirits want to take advantage of things like this. If they see a chance, they'll take it. They'll say anything, pretend to be anyone. It's why it's such a delicate and protected practice—or at least, why it should be."

I blink, processing what Valerie is saying. "That's...ominous. And vaguely threatening." I lean closer to the phone. "Is there anything we can do?"

Valerie draws in a breath. "You might need to call in the big guns for this. The house probably needs a cleanse of some kind."

"So you believe she's really doing this?" Stevie asks.

"I mean, you guys saw her perform a ritual that you know she's done at Lo's house countless times, *and* there's some kind of paranormal presence there—you tell me," Valerie says, and Stevie and I wordlessly lock eyes, unease written all over her face.

12

STEVIE

Setting up Lo's house for our paranormal investigation—something I usually say with finger-quotes but might actually mean this time—is serious business.

Andrew and the twins had gone to work setting up cameras in each room while Lo and I were gone. The goal is to capture anything that happens tonight. I'm on the fence about whether this will end up actually being worth it, but pretty much anything can be thrown together to look haunted. It just might not be the most exciting episode of television anyone's ever watched if most of what we do is add some disembodied voices in post-production.

The biggest difference between setting up Lo's house and setting up for all of our previous episodes is that we don't have to do any additional work besides cameras and mics. We don't have to worry about setting up a room a certain way, so we can capture a chair mysteriously falling or see a random flash of light.

This time, it'll just be us and the ghost that Lo seems pretty confident does, in fact, live in the house.

I can't bring myself to ask her how she's doing after all of the stuff with Sunniva. It's obvious it's been a lot for her to process. On the way back, she was the quietest I've heard her. As a professional paranormal encounter faker, I'm pretty certain Sunniva was fucking with all of us, and none of it was real.

There's only a tiny—a very, *very* tiny—part of me that believes that maybe there's more to the story than just clever set design. I still can't figure out how she could get a rock to move on its own.

After checking in on the cameras, the guys and I wait for nightfall. I find Lo in the kitchen, munching on a bag of chips from Trader Joe's, staring off in the distance.

"I hope you're not staring at some kind of figure in the corner," I joke, hoping to lighten the mood even a small amount. We've only known each other a short time, so it's hard to know what she needs. Everyone grieves differently. And I'm fortunate to have not lost any of my family members I've been close to, so I can't even attempt to connect to her on what she's gone through.

"No, just thinking," Lo says. She tightly wraps up the bag to close it up and latches a chip clip back onto it. "That whole thing was so weird. Everything with Sunniva, I mean. It's just not sitting right with me at all."

I lean onto her kitchen island. "It's not making sense to me, either."

"It felt...real, right?" she whispers, as if someone is going to come after her if they overhear. "Like, that actually happened?"

"I don't know," I say, and I really mean it this time. I've always been pretty firm in my beliefs. My grandparents and their neighbors love to share stories about encounters in the desert, but that's all they've ever been to me—stories. They're folklore.

But it's harder to convince myself when it's something that's actually happened to me. Discrediting the story of another person is one thing, but doing it to myself over something I saw with my own two eyes is another.

"I don't know," I admit. We're quiet for a beat. "Are you good for today? You don't have to stick this out with us. You've already had a long day."

"I'm alright," Lo says. Then she says, "That's a lie. I'm not. But I can handle this. We've made it this far already—I want to commit."

"You don't have to."

Lo shrugs. "I kind of want to see what evil spirit Sunniva might've brought into this house."

I nod and tap my fingers against her butcher block counter. "And you're...okay?"

She takes a deep breath. "I don't know. I just know I miss my mom, and seeing someone else have all those same feelings...it was really intense. I'll be bringing it up in therapy."

"I'm really sorry for your loss," I say. "I don't know if that's the right thing to say or if that's more annoying than anything to hear, but—"

"It's okay. There's not really a right thing to say. Nothing's ever going to make it better," she says. Her eyes flick up to meet mine, and nerves buzz in my chest. It's almost stupid how beautiful she is. "But I appreciate it."

"Yeah, of course." I avert my gaze and clear my throat. "Tonight should be interesting, whether anything actually happens or not."

"I agree. I'm kind of hoping the ghost shows out—I need proof of everything that's been going on here."

I chuckle. "I guess we'll see what happens."

We play the waiting game until the sun finally goes all the way down and it's dark enough to film. I settle onto the dining room table to catch up on the edits I didn't do last night while Lo gets comfortable on the couch.

After an hour of comfortable silence, I glance over in Lo's direction. She's typing away on her phone, her attention so focused on it that she doesn't realize I'm looking at her.

It's impossible not to imagine that the person on the other end of the phone is a fling of some kind. Despite agreeing that it was a one-time thing and definitely a moment of weakness, our time together keeps popping back up in my mind. I hear her breath in my ear, the sound of my name on her tongue. When I was driving us around earlier, it was so easy for me to remember what her touch felt like.

I look away, shaking my head. I can't fixate on her, can't let this become more than what it is. Or was.

We're going to film the rest of the episode, and I'm going to be entirely normal about it. And then I'm going to continue to be very normal about it even after we say goodbye, and I have to pretend that I don't want to see her again.

Even as I'm silently saying my goodbye to Lo, there's a small part of me that wonders why we even have to keep it to one time. We live in the same city; we can theoretically see each other whenever.

But there's no way with the work that we do, we'd ever been in the same place enough for that. And we might as well be in a long-distance relationship with how long it'd take to get to each other.

And beyond all of that, Lo was the one who'd made it clear it was a one-time thing. I'm not going to be the idiot who ignores her saying that and then gets hurt when she doesn't want anything more from me than something casual.

Even if there's a part of me that's hoping, maybe, she'll change her mind.

The front door suddenly flies open, making me and Lo jump. Lo's house has been suspiciously quiet all day—so quiet that we haven't had a single scare since we arrived back from Sunniva's. It's suspiciously quiet, and despite my best efforts, I'm on edge and waiting for the next weird thing to happen.

Not that I think the house might actually be haunted or anything.

"We come bearing enough food to feed a small city," Andrew says as he steps inside the house. The twins follow behind. All three of them are carrying a bag of fast food that's practically bursting at the seams.

"Jesus, did you guys buy the entire place out?" I shut my laptop—there's no chance I have any work left in me. It's been demonstrated to be impossible to focus when Lo is anywhere in my vicinity.

"Brain food."

"Right," I say, and clear my stuff from the table so we can lay the food out.

"We got everything everyone requested," Andrew says. He lugs his bag up onto the dining room table and starts pulling it out. Lo disappears into the kitchen, and the clattering of plates sounds out moments later.

"And everything else on the menu, too, apparently. You know our food budget isn't *unlimited* just because we've been writing these meals off, right?"

"Is that legal?" Lo asks as she comes back into the dining room with plates in hand.

"Don't come to me for tax advice. I still can't afford an accountant, so it's just been me, TurboTax, and whatever I want to write off on my taxes for years," I say, putting my hands up defensively. "Not one receipt from travel kept."

Lo snorts as she moves the food Andrew has been laying out on the table onto plates. After doing that, she moves on to placing all of the drinks onto coasters. When she catches me watching her with an amused smile, she blushes. "It's...real wood," she explains, almost like she's making a confession. "It's thrifted, at least."

"No judgment from me," I say, even though the mental math I'm doing on getting a real wood table of this size suggests this piece of furniture was *not* cheap. But I guess the same goes for all of the furniture in Lo's house. I don't know much about furniture, but I do know none of the furniture here is from IKEA; the show she was on had definitely paid her well.

The twins reach over Andrew to grab their food and settle into seats around the table. "Tonight's going to be crazy," Sean says, his mouth half-full.

"What makes you say that?" I ask, and Andrew hands me the plate of my food. We'd all agreed on a burger place nearby that Lo had recommended. I'd gotten a mushroom burger—my favorite—and fries. Lo kept it simple with her burger but ordered sweet potato fries. I can tell I'm smitten because just her liking sweet potatoes is cute to me.

He furrows his brow. "You didn't hear all of the shit going on?"

Lo and I look at each other. "No?"

"There was, like, a scratching sound or something in the walls."

"It was so loud. We heard it the entire time we were setting up cameras earlier," Tanner chimes in and stuffs a fry in his mouth.

Lo goes so pale she's practically a ghost herself. "What?" Her voice comes out small. "While we were gone?"

"Yeah. It was *crazy*," Sean says.

We all go so quiet we can hear a pin drop. Lo doesn't touch her food at all; she just stares at it, her thousand-yard stare suggesting she's not even on this planet with us anymore.

After another beat, Andrew sighs. "They're fucking with you," he says, and Tanner and Sean burst out laughing.

I throw my hands up, looking over in Lo's direction to make sure she's okay and still breathing. "Dude, what the fuck?"

Sean shrugs. "I saw an opportunity."

"You guys scared the shit out of me," Lo says, putting her hand to her chest. "Oh my god. I thought that was about to legitimately trigger a panic attack. That's the scariest thing I've ever heard." She laughs, the color slowly returning to her face.

"Not cool," I emphasize. I know Lo is too nice to bitch them out for that even though they deserve it.

"Sorry, that was mostly meant for Stevie—didn't mean to scare you, too," Sean says and I flip him off.

"Yeah, you're honestly really cool," Tanner says. He says it like a little brother who has just met his older sibling's friend. I'm glad both he and his brother are starting to take the hint that Lo is off-limits, even to their little schoolboy brains. But I wouldn't be surprised if part of that has to do with Andrew saying something to them; none of us have ever been particularly good at keeping secrets from each other.

"I'll take it," Lo says, sounding very much like the older sibling's friend who thinks anyone under the age of twenty-one might as well be an infant. I smile a little bit.

“It’s been kind of fun hanging out with someone new. We never really get to work with anyone outside of the three of us,” Sean says.

“Oh, yeah?” Lo glances over at me.

“We don’t usually engage with the talent, you know how it is,” I reply, mostly joking.

“Of course.” Lo smiles.

“But you can come investigate with us whenever,” Sean says. “You’re, like, really cool.”

“Yeah, this has been kind of sick,” Tanner agrees. “Stevie’s never been this nice to us before.”

I toss a fry at him. “Shut up,” I say, hoping my mock-annoyance will overshadow my embarrassment at getting called out like that.

“Thanks, guys,” Lo says, and I can tell she really means it. Her face softens as she shyly looks down at what’s left of the food in front of her.

There’s something about Lo’s soft smile and the warm, slightly dimmed light in the room that makes my heart ache. I can’t take a picture, but I want to. The best alternative I can come up with is staring at her, committing every single detail to memory—the way she’s leaning her head on her palm, one of her knees lifted up onto her chair, her hair pushed behind her ears.

A noise from across the house pulls me away. We all jump at the same time, turning to look at where it might’ve come from.

“What was that?” Andrew asks.

"Did you guys leave a window open or something when you were setting up?" I ask, thinking through possible options—a camera fell because it wasn't put up properly, the wind blew something over.

"I didn't open any in the first place," Andrew says. The twins shake their heads to confirm they didn't either.

Another sudden sound—the same thump from the same part of the house—makes all of us jump.

"What the fuck?" Sean whispers.

I look at Sean and Tanner. "Are you fucking with us again?" But when the boys shake their heads, just as startled as we are, I know they're telling the truth. "Are the cameras working?" I ask, my stomach at my feet. Lo has gone completely pale all over again.

"We can check," Andrew says. The thumping from the other room keeps going as he pulls out his laptop from his bag.

My immediate instinct is that we shouldn't be here. I'm not easily scared, but I don't fuck with an unexplained sound that seems almost like it's from a human. Every cell in my body wants to run.

But instead, I grip my thighs to keep myself grounded and take deep, intentional breaths.

Andrew starts up his laptop, the whole process taking what seems like a hundred years. His hands are shaking so much that he keeps pressing all the wrong keys. After three attempts at inputting his password, he closes his eyes and inhales before trying again. His hands are still shaking, but they're level enough that he's finally able to get it right this time.

I cautiously stand up and walk behind him to see what's on his screen. I know we could just walk to the other room to see it, but I can't bring myself to do it. Whatever is going on in that room is *loud*. Almost to the point that it seems like something living is in there.

Lo and the twins join me, and everyone pushed together to look over Andrew's shoulder. We normally don't look at live footage, but we also never have an excuse to check the cameras before. Even when we've filmed at abandoned hospitals and schools, we can always tell when a sound is just an animal or a creak from the building being old.

"Okay," Andrew says under his breath, as if he's bracing himself. His cursor hovers over the program we use to record and store our live footage.

Despite my historic impatience, even I can't bring myself to click on it for him. I'm stuck between wanting to know—desperate for some kind of explanation that makes us all laugh—and not wanting to be haunted forever by whatever the answer is.

I look next to me and see that Lo has her eyes half-closed, like we're watching a scary movie. When she sees that I'm looking at her, she ducks her head close to my shoulder and tucks her face in. Despite my lifelong love for horror, I've never done a horror movie date with a girl; I'm imagining this is a similar experience.

And, admittedly, I'm not hating it.

Knowing that Lo is scared makes me feel *less* scared, like my instinct to protect her is stronger than any fear I might be experiencing.

"Open it, Andrew," I say. I feel like we've been standing here forever, but the clock on Andrew's computer has only ticked up by one more minute.

Andrew makes a half-whining sound in protest. Still, across the house, the thumping continues. Whatever is causing it is either oblivious to us talking about it or doesn't care. "Okay. *Okay*. Fine." Andrew shakes out his shoulders and then finally clicks onto the app.

At first, it seems like everything is fine. I can see us crowded over Andrew's computer in one of the screens. There's the empty kitchen, the empty living room, and the guest room. I don't see anything that explains the sound we're hearing.

Lo inhales sharply and grips my arm. "Oh my god," she says.

"What? What are you looking at?" I ask, leaning in closer. Then, I see it.

In Lo's room, there are at least fifteen books scattered on the floor. Andrew clicks on the window to make it larger, and everyone leans in closer to see.

With the larger screen, we can now clearly see books flying off the shelves. They're coming off one by one—not in any particular rhythm and not with any specific order.

"Dude, what the fuck?" Tanner whispers.

I glance up at Lo's bedroom door, wondering what the hell is waiting for us just down the hall.

"I hate that. Whatever is going on in there is just..." Lo says, shaking her head. "Absolutely not."

"That's like something straight out of Paranormal Activity. That's crazy," Andrew says, voice full of awe. He's seemingly the only one of us who isn't scared anymore. Even the twins look uneasy, glancing between each other and then looking at the front door like they're debating on running. "We should go take a look."

"No, we shouldn't," I say quickly, even though I know he's right. The whole point of doing this is to investigate, even if I can't find a single logical explanation behind what I'm seeing.

"But it's kind of...surreal, right? Like it doesn't feel like it's actually happening," Andrew says. "I need to go see it for myself."

I take a deep breath. Even though I don't want to, I also don't want to admit that I'm scared. If Andrew's able to get his shit together and embrace that we're actually doing some paranormal investigative work instead of faking it, I can too.

"Alright, yeah. Let's go take a look," I say. "It's probably nothing, anyway."

I head to the archway between the dining room and kitchen, and everyone follows behind. As the five of us walk down the hall toward Lo's bedroom, I tell myself over and over again that it really will be nothing. I can't think of an explanation as to why Lo's books would be literally flying off the shelves, but I'm not about to immediately fall back on it being because of a ghost.

The sound doesn't slow down at all, even as we approach the door to Lo's room. It's a steady rhythm—books flying from the shelves into the wall across the room and then falling to the floor.

"I don't get why it keeps going after my books," Lo whispers, as if that'll make a difference in a paranormal being overhearing our conversation. Based on the stories I'd heard from my grandparents, it might as well know what Lo is thinking and feeling before she even knows.

From what I can tell, it's annoying to her that her books keep getting victimized, it's cute how strongly she feels about them. Even though I can't see her well in the dark light of the house, I can imagine the scrunch of her nose and the downturn of her lips.

When we make it to the bedroom door, I know there's no point in putting off the inevitable. I take a deep breath, close one of my eyes as if that'll protect me from what's inside, and then push the bedroom door open.

Predictably, there's no one.

We look at the books on the floor and the empty gaps in the bookshelf. The books weren't cleared one at a time, shelf-by-shelf; they were picked at random.

It's quiet for a beat. None of us move, and no more books go flying.

After long enough, Lo sighs—more with annoyance than anything. "You are the *worst*," she mutters. She squats down and picks up the books from the floor. "Nothing but a nuisance the entire time I've lived here."

"Are you shit talking the ghost right now?" Andrew asks.

"This isn't the first time we've bickered," Lo says.

"Do you need help?" I ask and walk over to help her pick up her books. I pick up a few off the ground, and Lo scowls.

"You guys were wondering why I wasn't that scared of my ghost before, and this is exactly why. Constantly doing things that are just annoying—"

"Stevie!"

I look over in Andrew's direction and just narrowly miss being hit by another book. "Oh, *shit*." I look at the book that's since hit the wall and fallen on the floor, and then look back over at the bookshelf as if there will be any kind of explanation.

Lo gasps, a hand to her heart. "Oh my god."

My heart is beating so fast I can hear the blood pounding in my ears.

"Sorry, maybe I shouldn't be so vocal. The ghost has been kind of agitated lately," Lo says sympathetically and gingerly touches my head as if the book actually hit me.

I laugh, but it comes across as more of a nervous chuckle. "It's alright."

"Good footage for the episode."

I nod, doing everything I can to bring my heart rate back down to normal. I might as well have just run the mile. "Good footage for the episode."

"Andrew, grab the camera. I know we weren't planning on starting yet, but we might as well," I say. I stack up the books of Lo's that are within reach, and Lo does the same.

"You got it." Andrew hurries down the hallway again so quickly that I can literally hear him running through the house.

I get up and walk over to the shelves to investigate. The most defiant part of myself wants to poke a hole in the story. There has to be a string attached to some of the books or *something*, but I can't think of anything. There's nothing hanging from the ceiling, and a setup for something like this would be too elaborate to set up in a few hours, even for someone as practiced as Andrew.

Andrew comes in with the camera, fumbling with it as he points it at me. There are times when being a low-budget, low-brow show has worked for us, like now. Our fans in particular have liked the almost found-footage way we shoot. We've never actually had to shoot with live-time urgency before—we'd only ever just pretended it was before—but it's turning out to be useful now to be able to basically just whip out a camera and go, like we're a news crew on the ground.

Andrew points at me to tell me that he's rolling. "We're in Lo's room right now, where we just caught books flying off the walls on camera." I wave my hand through the air near the shelves. "You can see that there aren't any strings. There's nothing built into the room to make the books randomly come down."

Talking about it on camera immediately brings me back into the headspace of filming our previous episodes. It makes it easier to separate myself from what's actually going on and instead think of it as an elaborate set design. It's all just beats I have to hit to tell a good story in the episode. Nothing more.

"This room has been a hotspot in the time we've been here, but Lo has told us previously that her bedroom has been off-limits. It's a new—and frightening—development," I continue and then motion for Andrew to cut.

"That was crazy, dude," Andrew says, almost giddy. "Like, the coolest thing I've ever seen."

"I don't know about *coolest.*" I move around some of Lo's books on the shelves, as if testing to see if any of them will suddenly go flying off. "I don't see what reason there would be to do something like that. Is it meant to be a threat? Or are we just being fucked with?"

"You're starting to sound like you might believe it's a ghost," Lo says from across the room.

I shrug off the comment, too proud to admit that this has been the strongest evidence so far that something might be going on. There are too many things piling up for it all to be coincidences. Blaming things on a house being old or the wiring being shitty or someone pulling a prank on us is one thing, but this doesn't feel like that anymore.

But the reality is that maybe all this time I've spent rolling my eyes at my grandparents and poking holes in stories about paranormal encounters and profiting off the curiosity of those who really want answers has been misguided. Maybe there has always been some truth to it all, and I just refused to see it.

I swallow hard. I'm not ready to deal with that yet. Not while I'm in Lo's house and potentially brushing shoulders with a ghost.

"Where to next, boss?" Andrew asks.

"I'm not sure—"

A book suddenly goes whizzing past my head, followed by another past my feet. I jump nearly a foot into the air. "Dude, what the fuck—"

"Move!" Lo shouts.

Andrew and I listen, jumping out of the way as one of Lo's bookshelves tips and then falls, crashing to the floor.

All of us scream—even the twins who are across the room—and jump back toward the door. Andrew grips the camera as he moves across the room in three giant steps.

I reach for Lo. "Are you okay?"

"I'm fine—are *you* okay? You were almost under it."

"Yeah, I'm good," I say and shake off the jolt of adrenaline that just jump-started my entire nervous system.

"I saw it swaying, like someone was trying to tip it. We'll have to check if the camera caught that—I'm sure it's even scarier to watch from a different angle," Lo says. "I almost thought I was making it up."

"I'm personally glad you said something," Andrew says.

I walk over to see if I can lift the bookshelf myself, and Lo shakes her head. "Don't even bother. I'll get it put back up soon.

And probably actually mount the shelves to the wall like I was supposed to do initially. Realizing now why it's important to do that."

"Because a ghost might knock it over?" I ask dryly.

"Exactly."

"I'm starting to think you should've called a priest instead of us," Sean murmurs warily.

"Me too," Lo admits.

A rustling sound outside pulls our attention to the closed bedroom window. Lo's curtains are open, but it's dark outside, so I can't see anything. But the way we all looked makes it clear I didn't just imagine how loud the sound was—or how close it was to us.

"What now?" Lo groans.

The sound continues. The hair on the back of my neck stands up immediately. Even though I can't see outside, an instinct in me of some kind is telling me that something is *definitely* looking back at us.

"*Shit*," I whisper, shaking out my shoulders.

Lo glances over at me. "You're not allowed to be scared. I need one of us to stay calm."

"I'm not scared," I lie, tilting my chin up. "And I think Andrew is the one who wants to take the lead on this. I might as well let him."

"Right. Because he's showing initiative and not because you're too scared to go look at what might be outside."

"Exactly."

Lo's lips turn up. I can see in the quiver of her hand that she's unsettled, but it's nice to have even a second where I can forget that we're in the middle of our own personal horror movie.

What sounds like someone scratching at the exterior walls of the house sounds out, immediately killing the playful mood.

"Oh hell no." Tanner puts his hands up. "I didn't think we'd have to deal with a ghost that can go outside of the house, too. That's fucked up."

"It could just be an animal or something." But even as I say it, I'm not convinced. It would have to be a *massive* animal for it to make that kind of sound and have it carry through the house. It's like someone is fully ripping at the siding, scratching all the way down it.

Andrew perks up, "Shit, we didn't set up a camera back there—I'm gonna go see if I can catch anything out there."

"I don't know if that's smart," Lo says. "I know we're investigating ghosts or whatever, but that could very well be an animal. Or a human. Which is arguably much scarier."

"It'll be fine—Sean, come with me."

"What the fuck? You're not leaving me in this house," Tanner says. "I'm coming too."

"Whatever, just hurry—we have to catch it before it stops." Andrew adjusts the camera on his shoulder and heads for the back door. The twins follow closely behind.

"Men," Lo says, throwing her hands up.

With the three of them gone, the house feels eerily quiet. I grip the flashlight, bracing myself for something else to happen.

"Is it weird of me to say that I find this...kind of fun? Even though I'm scared out of my mind?" Lo whispers. "I think I finally understand the appeal of haunted houses at carnivals."

I snort. "I think it might only be fun right now because nothing is happening. Give it a minute and you'll probably feel differently."

"Don't jinx us. I don't want anything else happening tonight. I'll be perfectly happy never having another ghostly encounter in my own house again."

I don't state the obvious—there's no way the night is over.

The voices of Andrew and the twins carry through the closed window, muffled and a little bit distant. The sound has slowed down since they went out, but that's not to say that nothing weird is going on.

"We need to get walkie-talkies or something. I don't like that they're out there." I wipe my hands off on my jeans, looking around.

"You don't want to call them?"

"Phones take away from the vibe on screen. We're going for a particular atmosphere here."

Lo's lips turn up in an amused smile. "No, of course. Why didn't I think of that?"

"*Lauren*."

My blood runs cold. The voice doesn't feel human—it's too low, too much of a whisper. It comes across like nothing more than a breeze passing through the room.

Lo slowly turns to look at me. "Was that you? Please tell me that was you."

I shake my head. I want to chalk it up to me hearing things, my mind playing tricks in the dark, but we heard it at exactly the same time.

"And the boys aren't back inside? This isn't another prank?"

"I haven't heard them come back in, and they're not particularly quiet," I say. In fact, I haven't heard any of them at all in a second. It's gotten suspiciously silent.

"Hello?" I call out. I wait a beat to see if anything else happens.

"Did you also hear it say my name?" Lo asks, her hand finding my arm again as she ducks behind me. "Also, using my legal name is an insane choice. It's like I'm being haunted by my grandma."

"I guess the odds are never zero, considering Sunniva seems to have spoken to every dead person in Southern California."

I shiver all over again thinking about what we saw earlier at Sunniva's house. I earnestly don't know what's scarier—being able to actually invite a ghost into her house, or convincing everyone around her that she's able to do it.

I sigh, annoyed all over again that I keep getting scared so easily. "Are you still there? We're waiting," I call out again, pointing the flashlight toward Lo's bedroom door. The hallway, even when illuminated, is eerie at night.

"Why did you buy this house again?"

"Natural light. And location."

"Did you take into consideration that this place is really unsettling when the lights are out?"

"Major selling point for me, actually. The ghost, too," Lo says. "And it's not that bad. Every house looks scary in the dark."

"Not like this," I say. The last time I'd been to a place that made me this uneasy was when I was a kid visiting my grandparents. I'd refuse to leave my bedroom after a certain hour, even to use the bathroom, because I was so certain something was going to be waiting for me out there. The visceral memory surprises me—I haven't thought about what it was really like staying at their house in a long time. I've spent so long using it as a form of credibility, like proximity to creepy desert lore is enough to make me an expert, that I forget the things that I saw and felt actually happened.

And after a lifetime of downplaying it, I'm starting to think maybe my grandparents weren't wrong when they said there was something strange about their town.

"I know I've asked before, but is my house really that bad? Compared to all of the other places you've been, I mean. Now that you're seeing all of this."

"Yes," I say, knowing there's no use in lying. Lo could go back and watch any of our old episodes to easily confirm it. Even the fake ghost encounters we've set up for the camera haven't been this elaborate. It's the dilemma of truth being stranger than fiction—we don't want to risk going too far and people assuming it's all made up. But we've never been in the situation of *actually* catching paranormal activity on camera, so I don't know how any of this will play out for fans. It's not like I can go on camera and say *this is the house that made me realize we don't* have *to fake our show.*

Lo bites her lip. "Maybe it's not worth it to try staying here."

"Not into the looming threat of a bookshelf being pushed onto you at any point?"

"Not particularly—"

"*Lauren.*"

We both go completely still. This time, there's no use in getting confirmation from each other.

"Why does it want me?" Lo whispers. She's gripping my arm so hard that I'm certain there will be bruises left behind by her fingers.

I bite my lip, wishing I had something helpful to offer. But I don't. "I don't know."

"I know enough to know I'm not supposed to go to the source of the sound," Lo says. "Did your paranormal investigator school teach you what to do if a ghost wants to kill you?"

"There's no paranormal investigator school. And no, that's not really our deal."

"You guys continue to be useless."

"Keyword—*investigator.*"

"All I'm hearing is—"

"*Lauren.*"

I put my hands up to my ears like a bug just buzzed past me, and drop my head. The voice was so close this time that it felt almost like it was in the room with us. It might as well have been standing right next to me.

My stomach sinks. If the sound is that close, that must mean the source of the sound is in here with us.

"We need to get out of here," I say.

Lo glances over at me, slowly dropping her hands from her ears. She has the same expression on her face as me. "Yes, definitely."

We clear out of the room as quickly as we can. I don't even bother looking around to see if there's anything—or anyone—actually in the room. I'm assuming we probably wouldn't be able to see it anyway, if there was, since that seems to be a trend around here.

We cut back down the hallway and go toward the kitchen. This room feels even more vulnerable than the bedroom—it has entry points from pretty much every direction and windows leading to the outside.

"Any sign of them?" I ask, even though it's obvious Andrew and the twins aren't within view. Where the hell did they end up?

Lo shakes her head. She blinks nervously, looking around the kitchen. I sign my flashlight in the opposite direction, checking the perimeter.

"What if something..." Lo starts and then stops.

"It didn't," I insist way too quickly. My gut feeling, based on knowing them for so long, is that they're just off being idiots somewhere. But the odds aren't exactly zero that something bad did happen to them.

"Maybe they ended up out front?"

"Okay," Lo agrees.

With the flashlight illuminating our walk through Lo's house, we make it back to the living room. Even though I know we would've heard if the boys were in here, my stomach sinks when I see that the room is empty.

I walk over to the window to peek outside, cutting the flashlight for a second so there's no glare. "I don't think I see them." I sigh. "Where the hell would they have gone? It's not like you have a huge plot of land—no offense."

I pull my phone from my pocket and type out, *Where the hell are you guys?* And then send it in the group chat I have with them.

"So weird. Maybe they're pulling another prank. But it feels a little early in the night for that—and poorly planned considering there's more than enough for them to film in here without extra bullshit."

I realize then that my investigative partner has been quieter than she's ever been in the admittedly very brief time I've known her. "Lo?" I turn the flashlight back on and face it toward her.

Her eyes are wide with panic. "Stevie, I can't—" Lo points to her neck. Her voice is strained. "I can't breathe."

I hurry over to her. "What do you mean?"

"Pressure." She huffs the word out through labored breaths. There's a look of genuine fear in her eyes that scares me.

"What's going on?" I ask, gently touching her shoulders, then her neck. "Panic attack? How can I help?"

"Get...its...hands...off...my...neck." Lo fights for every word, pushing them out with force. She claws at her throat, desperate now.

"I don't see anything," I say frantically. I put my flashlight between my teeth and reach for her neck, looking for any way to possibly help her.

Lo screams in frustration. "Get...off of me!"

I know the comment isn't directed at me based on the way she's staring up at the ceiling and looking around the room.

I bring the flashlight up to her, careful not to get it in her eyes. When I see her throat tensing—literally held tight like someone is actively squeezing it—I nearly drop the flashlight.

Reality sinks—we're not protected from a murderous ghost just because we're here investigating. If all of the other things that have been happening have been ways of scaring us and attempts at hurting us—or worse—then this is not looking good.

And might also offer some insight into why I haven't heard anything from the boys in what feels like a suspiciously long time.

"*Shit.*" I look around the room for something, anything, that can help. But what the hell am I going to use on a hand that doesn't exist?

I take a deep breath, trying not to completely freak out and make things worse for Lo.

"Let her go!" I shout.

Lo's face is turning red now. I move the flashlight in a one-eighty to see if maybe whatever is doing this has some kind of physical form. I don't exactly know what the fuck fighting a ghost off would entail, but I would figure it out for Lo.

"Stevie." Lo's eyes well with tears.

A chill cuts through the room, making my blood turn to ice. My mouth goes dry with fear. The temperature drops in LA in the late fall, but never like that. There's not a breeze in the world that could explain what just passed through me.

It clicks into place all at once—I don't even have to turn around to know something is looking at us. But I do it anyway, desperate to prove to myself that there isn't. My least favorite feeling is being proven wrong, but right now, I'd take that a million times over being right that *something* is in this house.

I take shallow, shaky breaths as I bring my flashlight around.

The light trails over Lo's furniture—her couch, coffee table, and fireplace. And then, tucked back in the corner between the living room and dining room, is something so unexpected I nearly drop my flashlight.

I keep my flashlight fixed on *it*, whatever the hell it is—this *figure* who has to be at least seven feet tall. It's human-like but simultaneously not. It's too thin, too tall, too shadowy. I can see it in front of me, but I also feel like I could put my hand through it if I really wanted to. But I know better than to try that.

Lo suddenly drops to her knees. She gasps for air, as if whatever I'm looking at has finally let go.

It takes a beat for my brain to process. As soon as it sinks in, I'm gripped with a kind of fear that I've never felt before. Lo looks up at me, but I can't say anything. Fear has completely frozen me in place. She turns to look at what I'm looking at.

And then she screams, speaking for both of us.

13

LO

For the first time since moving into my haunted house, I scream.

It's a deep-from-my-gut scream that barely sounds like it's coming from my own body. My throat burns, and the air feels physically squeezed out of my lungs. I scream until I don't have any breath left and then keep going. I don't even know what I was screaming for or about; it isn't going to scare off whatever the fuck is standing in the corner in my living room. And I can't scream for help—Stevie is already here with me, in the same exact position as me, the only difference being that I'm frozen in place on the floor and Stevie is scrambling for the door.

As soon as she realizes I can't move, she comes back and pulls me up from the ground, yanking me to come with her. I don't know if I want to cover my eyes and pretend it isn't real or if I want to stare and make sense of what I'm looking at. The logical part of my brain is throwing out all kinds of options—a weird shadow, a trick of the eye. But I know the truth. I didn't make up getting choked. And I definitely didn't make up whatever the fuck Stevie's flashlight had found in my living room.

Getting one last look over my shoulder as Stevie physically drags me out of the room, I try to make sense of the figure. I will never forget what it looks like—the looming shadow, the distinctively human figure, the way it doesn't have any features that I can see, but I just *know* it's looking at me.

As we run, I move past the freeze phase and go onto something else entirely—a sickening, heavy feeling that makes me think I really might throw up. Or cry. Or maybe just scream some more.

"What the fuck was that!" I shouted. My chest heaves as we cut across the living room and go to the front door. I don't care if there's an episode to film or if this is the coward's way of handling things—I do *not* want to stick around here.

I reach for the handle and yank on it, but it won't budge. I try everything I can think of, using all of the muscle and strength I have. The handle is so stuck that it won't even turn; it's like someone is on the other side holding it in place.

"Oh my god," I whine, too scared to care about how pathetic I sound.

"Let me try," Stevie says and quickly takes my place. She does the same thing I did, desperately yanking on the door handle. She slaps her hand to the wood, either out of frustration or fear. I can't tell.

"We have to run. We're not getting out of here," Stevie says and takes my hand.

We scramble down the hallway, and I think over the options we have for safety. Is hiding in a closet enough to stop a ghost? In a bedroom with the door locked? The only solutions I can think of are more for slasher films than for something that has the ability to go through walls.

"Shit." Panic is taking over, and it's hard for me to think logically—or think at all. The only thing my brain is telling me to do is run. Leave it to Sunniva to somehow bring *the* scariest ghost ever into this house.

The kitchen offers the first hint of safety that I can think of. Something about being in a small, compact space feels safer than hiding in a giant room that allows a ghost ample opportunity to fuck with us.

I grab Stevie by the arm and go into the smallest enclosed area of the house—the pantry. I pull us both inside and then shut the door. It's dark and compact and clearly not meant for two full-sized adults to hide in, but it works fine enough. We sit down on the floor, and I pull my knees to my chest. Stevie's shoulder pressed against mine is a comforting reminder that I'm at least not doing this alone.

"Do you think it'll get us in here?" I whisper.

"I think our best bet is no longer being inside the house, but maybe that's just me," Stevie says dryly. It's so dark that I can't even make out my own hand in front of me, nonetheless Stevie's expression.

"But earnestly, do you think we'll be okay?" I ask. "Expert opinion."

"I'm sure we'll be fine—"

"I'd really like something more certain than that. Some facts or something. Like, oh, actually, ghosts *can't* come into pantries because it explicitly violates some kind of ghost code."

"I don't think that's how that works."

My heart rate isn't slowing down from when we were running earlier. If I keep this up, I'm going to start hyperventilating. "Please tell me something that will calm me down."

"It's...all imagination. It was a figure. We made it up. If we go back out there, nothing will happen to us," Stevie says like she's reading off of a list. There's a question marked tacked on at the end of each statement, like she's just trying different ones out to see what'll land.

I can make out Stevie's figure in the dark now, my eyes slowly adjusting. "Anything else?"

Stevie sighs and does the best she can by throwing her hands up in the tight space. "I don't really know."

"What, not used to comforting people during paranormal encounters? Everyone's too cool and experienced for that?"

"Uh, not necessarily? I guess?"

"Stevie, genuinely—what the *fuck* does that mean?"

"I—" she groans. "I'm not actually a paranormal investigator, okay?"

I blink, certain she's making some kind of joke. "So, what are you? Like, ghost hunter instead? It's all technicalities?"

"No, I mean, like, the show is usually fake. We do this all for TV. It's scripted." She sighs. "I—I'm sorry. I don't have anything to say because I don't know anything. None of it was ever real before this. I can't comfort you or myself or explain what's going on."

"What do you mean none of this is real?" I can feel my voice going shrill. I bring it back down to a whisper. "You don't actually know how to use any of the equipment? You're not actually tracking anything?"

"I don't know, it's all just been like...us. It's a producer thing. We buy shit from, like, Amazon. I kind of thought everyone knew these shows were staged, at least to a certain degree."

"No! I messaged you because I thought you could actually help me!" I put my hands to my face and groan. "You've got to be fucking kidding me."

"I mean, we didn't really *have* to lie to you. The only thing we lied about was that we'd had experience ghost hunting before. But even then, I don't think we ever claimed to be, like, experts or anything—"

"Using that you lied by omission as your defense right now is *not* helping your case." I shake my head. "God, this is so *annoying*. So you guys are just as oblivious as I am? You literally don't know anything?"

"I guess we've learned some stuff over the years but not, like, a lot," Stevie says, letting her sentence fade out. When she sees the expression on my face, she quickly presses her lips together. "I'm sorry we lied, okay? But everything that's been happening here is one hundred percent real. We're not causing any of this. We might've lied a little bit—"

"More than a little bit! And to a whole lot of people!"

"Okay, we might've lied—*period*—but it was never meant to hurt you. We just knew the exposure would be good for our show. We weren't expecting your house to actually be haunted. But I do think this has changed things for us. I don't know if I'm really a believer now or not, but I am starting to think that there's more to this show than us having to fake everything."

I tilt my head against the wall, staring up at the ceiling of the closet. "Oh my god." I take a deep breath. "You're taking advantage of people. You're like who I thought Sunniva was before she actually did bring a ghost into the house."

Stevie's quiet for a beat. "Ouch," she says. It's so genuine that I immediately feel bad for throwing a stone like that. "You really think I'm like Sunniva?"

I take a breath and then sigh. "No. I don't think you are. You're both doing it for money, but she's intentionally taking money from people who are grieving."

"We're also definitely not making nearly as much money from lying as Sunniva is," Stevie says, and I exhale the world's smallest laugh through my nose. "I can't tell if I'm making it better or worse," she says.

"I can't either," I admit, throwing my hands up. I take in everything Stevie's saying, trying to think about it objectively. I can see where she's coming from—I am great exposure. My name carries weight. And even though I wished they'd told me from the beginning they weren't actually ghost hunters, it hasn't really caused *me* any direct harm. I also can't fault someone in what is technically reality TV for tricking me—that's kind of their whole shtick.

I also always knew, even before meeting them, that a ghost hunter wasn't going to be able to get rid of my ghost; all they'd ever do is confirm that there is one. And enough has happened in my house to confirm that even without the help of fancy technology and a team of actual paranormal investigators. It's the classic issue of someone doing a math problem wrong but still somehow finding the right answer.

"Are you mad at me?" Stevie asks.

"I don't know," I say and then sigh. "No. I'm not. I might be annoyed, but I'm finding it really hard to be mad at you right now, even if you did lie to me."

Maybe I'm too forgiving by nature or maybe Stevie is just really hot or maybe this whole thing has been too scary to ever let anything bother me again, but I can't bring myself to hold a grudge.

"It wasn't intentional. And that'll be my last lie. I promise," Stevie says. She sticks out her pinkie finger. "*First* and last."

I look at her face and then down at her hand. I bite back a smile as I loop my pinkie around hers. "You are so annoying."

"It's show-biz, baby," Stevie says. I can tell from her tone that she's trying to make me laugh and, unfortunately, it works. "I really am sorry. If it makes you feel any better, all of this shit that happened is making me realize we might've not needed to fake our show this whole time."

I turn and look at her. "Are you, Stevie Anderson, telling me you believe in ghosts now?"

"Whatever," Stevie says, leaning away from me.

I pull her back toward me by her arm. "*Finally*," I say, and Stevie chuckles.

Because the pantry doesn't get any natural light, I keep an eye on the weather app all night—waiting and waiting and waiting for the time it says the sunrise is supposed to start. Stevie is asleep with her head propped up on my shoulder. We've only been in here for an hour or two, but it feels like centuries. The adrenaline is still pumping through me, keeping me too alert to relax.

"Stevie, the sun is up," I whisper. I jostle her on my shoulder to wake her up without scaring her.

She lifts her head and I can see her processing everything—that she's awake, that I'm here, that we're in a tiny dark room. She puts her hand to the pantry wall as if to check that it's real.

"None of that was a dream," she mumbles.

"Unfortunately not."

We slowly emerge from the pantry, half-crawling because my legs have lost all circulation from being curled up so tightly all night. My muscles are screaming for help.

I look around, waiting for *something* to happen: something to fly off a wall or table, or a figure hovering nearby. I feel less like there's a ghost in the house and more like there's a killer waiting for me, like I'm in some kind of horror movie.

But there's nothing.

And then, after a beat and then two and then three, there's still nothing.

"Let's get out of here," I say. I half stumble to the door, my body temporarily having forgotten how to walk. Stevie follows behind me. She rolls out her shoulders and groans.

As I look around my now perfectly quiet and still house, I think about everything that unfolded last night. We'd gotten the first part of an answer—there's a ghost, and Sunniva definitely brought it into the house. But who is it? And why does it suddenly seem so agitated?

I want to know the whole truth. But I don't know if I have it in me to deep dive into it yet—this is, unfortunately, still my house. And after everything with Sunniva, I'm not sure I'm in the business of communicating with the dead. Either way, I'll have a whole lifetime to explore it. Ideally, with a priest next time.

And, just maybe, it'd be the perfect excuse to invite Stevie back for a second-part to our episode.

And the rest of the *Paranormal America* team, too. Obviously.

When we make it to the front door, I reach for the handle like it might burn me. Instead of being practically glued into place like it was last night, it's back to normal. It turns with ease.

As I push the door open to leave, Stevie and I look at each other. I almost ask her if we made the whole thing up, if it was some weird dream, but I resist. I don't think I want to know the answer.

The twins and Andrew are already outside when we get there, one of the twins napping in my small front yard.

"You guys good? We kept waiting for you guys to come out here and find us," Andrew says.

Stevie and I look at each other again. The night flashes before me—the fear, the screaming, the hiding. I don't know if I'll ever be able to step foot in this house comfortably ever again.

But here's Andrew and the twins in front of us, acting like nothing is wrong.

"You have no idea," I mumble.

"We're good," Stevie says slowly, her brow furrowed slightly.

"We're already packed up and ready to go. We got some *insane* footage from last night. I think this episode is going to be an absolute banger."

"Yeah," Stevie agrees. We look at each other again, part of me wondering if last night even really did happen or if it actually *was* all just some elaborate mutual nightmare.

But no—I know for certain it really did. Every second of it was horrible and completely unforgettable. It's the kind of night that changes a person fundamentally—the kind of night that really makes someone, even the most skeptical, believe that some things can't be easily explained away.

Stevie kicks Tanner's foot from where he's lying in the grass, and he jolts awake. He looks at Stevie and then at the rest of us heading out toward the van, startled. Stevie continues walking to the van, leaving Tanner to put the pieces together himself.

"We're finally leaving?" Tanner asks.

"We're finally leaving," Stevie teases over her shoulder.

"Oh, thank *god*." Tanner hops up from the grass.

The boys and Stevie load up the van with the last of their things and toss their backpacks inside. Andrew slams the back doors closed, and Stevie heads around to the front.

"You'll be around?" Stevie asks, looking at me.

"I was actually thinking I might spend some time in Topanga."

"Oh." Her eyebrows visibly shoot up with surprise.

"We'll see if those ghosts are a little more manageable than the one here," I say, only half-joking.

Stevie gets into the van and shuts the door. "We're shooting another episode soon—not in LA," she says. She has her arm over the side of the van window, her sunglasses hanging between her fingers. The early morning sun hits her face so beautifully, it makes my heart ache. I have to resist reaching out to touch her. "Just in case you're looking for an excuse to get away."

"I'll consider," I say, my arms propped up on the open window.

Stevie's lips twist into a smile. "Alright."

I take a beat, taking in her crooked, teasing smile and the comforting timbre of her voice. She hasn't even left yet, and I can already tell I'll miss her. "Bye, Stevie Anderson," I say and step back onto the sidewalk.

"Bye for now, Lo Lane."

Our eyes stay locked on each other for a beat longer than we should allow. Everything from the very brief time we spent together plays out in my mind—us first meeting, Stevie's annoyingly effortless charm winning me over, the way she stayed so level for me during everything with Sunniva, and then the scariest few hours of my life.

Our—admittedly perfect—night in the hotel.

Stevie starts up the van and asks her team if they want to go get breakfast somewhere. She holds up her hand in goodbye and then pulls away from my sidewalk, locking eyes with me in the side mirror a few times as she does. The last time we look at each other, I'm certain there's a smile on her lips.

I watch until the van completely disappears from sight, swallowed up by the other cars and suburban streets surrounding it.

Even as I watch her leave, I know this won't be the last time I see her.

Acknowledgements

I'm so incredibly fortunate that publishing a book is not something I have to do alone. While I do spend many, *many* quiet hours in front of a computer writing and plotting and rewriting and re-plotting, there are people kind enough to make every other step of the process a little less lonely.

A few of them, in no particular order:

Thank you to my readers who made writing a passion project possible. I went into publishing with the goal of writing books for myself, fairly certain it'd be hard to find people who'd want to read any of them. You've proven me wrong day after day and I don't have the words for how grateful I am.

Thank you to my editor, Emily Ladner, for being an absolute superstar and taking this book on without hesitation even though it's very different from *Tip In* (sorry for scaring you!!)

Thank you Caravelle Creates for the beautiful cover. It's magic how you'll turn a paragraph of random thoughts into something so perfect for the book.

Thank you to my PA, Carly, for your unwavering support and openness to any ideas I throw your way. I'm so, so grateful for everything you do.

Thank you Untold Stories for your social media support—I literally would not have any time left in the day if I had to do all of my social media posts on my own. You've saved me a million times over.

And thank you to my friends and family who are very patient with me despite constantly being on self-imposed deadlines. I love you all so much. Here's to the start of another series (I'm sorry).

Also by Josie Mae

Lakeside Green University:

Tip In

Bank Shot

Paranormal America:

With Spirit

About Josie

Josie Mae (she/her) is a lesbian who writes sapphic romance. She's a sports romance girl through and through despite being generally unathletic, and she says y'all far too much for being a city girl. She has worked a million odd jobs, lived a million different lives, and wants to live for a million more years. Josie writes all of her books with her small but mighty chiweenie, Baby Mae, by her side.